Fearful Farewell
by
David Cox

ALSO BY DAVID COX

NOVELS
The Old Must Die
Petrarchan Girl

SCREENPLAYS
Student Loaners
Return of the Devil
Curmudgeon
#Anhedonia

NONFICTION
Indie!

This is a work of fiction. Names, characters, places, and incidents are either the product of the author's imagination or are used fictitiously. Any resemblance to actual persons, living or dead, events, or locales, is entirely coincidental.

Slain Diamond Books

Copyright 2020 by David Cox
All rights reserved.
Printed in the United States of America

For the class of 2020

"The very meaninglessness of life forces man to create his own meanings."

Stanley Kubrick

Fearful Farewell

PART ONE

THE WAGES OF FEAR

SORCERER

1

"Why do you always think of other girls when we kiss?"

Her words stop me because she is right. No, I am not thinking of "other girls," but I am distracted. And she is the reason for my absence of mind.

"What are you talking about?" I ask with put-on bewilderment. "You know that I never think of other girls. Who could possibly make me look elsewhere?"

Brianna kisses me again and then leans back. The movie theater is completely dark except for the light pouring over the seats from the screen at the front. We are sitting in our usual seats, at the back of the theater and to the right. We are about as far away from the screen's light as one could possibly get, but that does not seem to stop Brianna's eyes from illuminating in the dark.

"Perhaps it would be that those other girls aren't leaving you behind," she replies.

She knows my weakness, because she is the bearer of them. It is her eyes. If I lock onto them, I completely fold as if I were on the back end of a thirty-six hour waterboarding session. I cannot lie when she locks eyes with me, as she is currently doing.

"That is still not enough of a reason for me," I answer sincerely.

"So what is it, Guy?" she asks, looking at me with her head tilted downward. She knows all the ways to get to me.

What am I supposed to do, though? She's so damned gorgeous. "Why are you so distracted?"

It is a completely fair question for her to ask her boyfriend of three years, but I do not want to tell her the truth. It will hurt too much and create an argument, and I just cannot handle arguing right now. I only want to enjoy my time with her. *My little-remaining time.*

I look away so I can successfully lie. "It's honestly nothing. I'm just thinking about the end of school."

"Guy, it's only Christmas," she states, as if I had somehow forgotten. "Why are you thinking about the end of school now? We're still months away."

"No, I know. It's just that… Don't you ever worry about what's next?"

"Well, of course I do. You know I do, but what good does that do now?"

"I dunno…"

Brianna evaluates my brilliant response. "It really is that, isn't it?"

"What?" I say.

"You think I'm leaving you behind," she says.

"No, I don't think that. I *know* that."

"Guy," Brianna stops me firmly.

"B," I reply back just as firmly.

"Why can't you just be honest with me? Isn't that what makes a successful couple? Isn't that why we have lasted so long while everyone else in our class can't date anyone longer than two months?"

She has a point, of course. Honesty is the most important factor in a relationship. But equally important is the ability to avoid a fight. And I have that ability all but mastered.

"I am being honest, B. I'm just thinking about graduation, this place, and what I'll have to do once summer comes. It's a lot to think about. I'm sorry for being distracted."

Brianna studies me, estimating my sincerity. I do not think I pass her test with high marks, but I do pass. "It'll be okay, Guy. I promise. It really will. I'll always be here."

"I promise that I'll never be distracted again while I am in your heavenly embrace," I murmur, attempting to entice her favor and, perhaps, land a kiss.

Instead, her face reveals repulsion for a moment – *just a moment* – but it hurts nonetheless. "Ew, did you really just say that?" she laughs.

I laugh too and point toward the screen. "It's these movies! How can you not start talking like them when you sit through as many as I do?"

"Fair point," she says, initiating the kiss this time. "Perhaps we need to take this conversation to a less-populated avenue?"

I look around the near-empty theater. "What could possibly be less populated than this place? The library? And why would you say it like that? A 'less-populated avenue'?" I laugh.

"Hey, these movies rub off on me, too. I may not sit through as many as you do, but I've endured my fair share."

"No, you're right, though. That sounds *really good*," I say in my best seductive voice, but then I pause.

She stands, begins to put on her coat, but stops when I do not follow suit. "What?"

I gesture toward the screen and shrug.

"We really have to finish this movie? You're choosing *it* over *me*?"

"No, I'm not choosing it 'over you', but we only have like thirty minutes left and I need to know if these guys get across that bridge with the nitroglycerin."

Brianna and I are at the near-end of a *The Wages of Fear*/*Sorcerer* double feature, something this theater specializes in. It is no wonder why either. As I look at the screen, I cannot help but be mesmerized. The truck is about to tip over on the wooden bridge in the middle of the rain storm in the jungle. Not only that, but the driver is about to run over his cohort, who has fallen through the rotten wood and is now nose-to-rubber with a massive, spinning tire. What other small town in Missouri shows movies like this William Friedkin masterpiece on the big screen?

Not a single one.

"Well, Guy, since this movie, the second in this double feature, is a remake of the first, I would say that you could probably piece it together. I'm guessing both movies end similarly."

I remain silent.

"Fine," she says. "We'll finish the movie. But I can't promise that I'll be in the mood afterwards."

I look at the screen, and then back at Brianna. And then back at the screen. "Screw it, let's go."

With that, I leave the theater, holding her hand.

Walking next to Brianna, and touching the skin on her hand, makes me happier than anything in the world. Even more than a classic double feature. But I am struggling today, and it all has to do with those comments she made earlier in the theater.

She assured me that she will "always be here."

That is the problem. She won't be.

In truth, my distraction all had to do with that fact. The reality of this moment terrifies me. I am beginning life and I am about to lose… *everything*. My best friend. My constant in life. My true love.

The thought makes me question everything in my life. Every plan I had previously made. Every decision I have been making for the past six months to set up my post-high school life. What is this all for? What does it mean? If I can't be with her, it seems pointless.

I know it seems childish to think this way. There is more to life than sustaining a relationship with one's "high school sweetheart." But she is all I have. Truly. Without her, I am destined to enter a world of loneliness and isolation, and I do not know if I will cope well in that kind of environment.

I want her in my life. *I need her in my life.*

And yet there is nothing I can do to stop her from leaving me.

2

"That was quicker than usual," Caitlyn says as I enter the theater's lobby the next day. She is hanging Christmas lights around the posters previewing our coming attractions, our concession stand counter, and our handmade "Bristol Arts Theater" sign that hangs above the ticketing counter. Caitlyn is passionate about many things in life, and Christmas just happens to provide her with one of those rare occasions in which she can be her true self without facing judgment.

"What do you mean?" I say as I hang my coat up on our employee rack, near the break room.

"Last night. I didn't expect you to get back so soon after you left with Brianna."

"That's not exactly what a guy wants to hear."

"I meant your *drive* to take her home," Caitlyn clarifies in a drawn-out "Oh, my gosh" sort of way. "I would've closed up for you if you didn't want to come back. I'm more than capable."

I love having Caitlyn as a coworker because she, in many ways, acts as my complete opposite. She is always happy, chipper, and gives people the benefit of the doubt. There is something incredibly refreshing about that, even if I do find it unrealistic and somewhat irresponsible.

"It really wasn't a big deal," I say as I join her behind the ticketing counter. "The roads had mostly cleared up by then. I appreciate it, though." I then fall into my usual position – elbows resting on the counter with my hands clasped together. I laboriously sigh.

"What's the matter?" Caitlyn asks. She pretends as though she is completely focused on her Christmas lights display, but I know she is more interested in my plight. *Or plights.*

"Nothing," I lie.

"Just tell me what it is," she sighs herself. "We both know you'll deny that there's a problem for a while, and then you'll do your droopy dog face again in about an hour, and then an hour after that, you'll finally tell me what's bothering you. So, can't we skip all of that? Our shift together ends in three hours, so that doesn't leave us much time for a full therapy session."

I stare ahead blankly. She is completely right, but I do not want to give her the satisfaction of knowing that exactly. It could lead to tricky territory. Before long, I will lose all autonomy... I will not know what is good for me at all. I will have to take all of my future problems to her as well, because she so successfully helped me with one of them. *This* problem.

Finally, I answer. "It's so close."

"The end of school?" Caitlyn replies, hanging her last strand of lights.

"Yeah," I confirm simply.

"You always make such a big deal of the small changes in your life."

"Um, usually I agree with everything you say, Caitlyn – *literally* everything – but this is not a small change. This is the biggest change of our lives. Maybe of any person's life. The step from being told what to do every moment of your day to absolute freedom, responsibility, and... *debt*. That's terrifying."

"It doesn't have to be, though."

"How can it not?" I scoff. "At least you get to leave this town."

Caitlyn turns her full attention to me because she knows that this is really my issue. *Leaving town.*

"Guy, you *can* leave," she says with reassuring eyes. "You absolutely do not have to stay here."

"I absolutely do," I retort. "And when I do, it's all over with us."

"Us?"

"I meant with Brianna and me, but yeah, us too," I say. "Everybody is going to leave me behind, and that'll be the end of that."

"You're so dramatic," she slugs me in the arm.

"No, I'm not," I answer defensively.

"Yes, you are. You act like my little brother. You have created this 'poor me' mentality, and I must say... it's not your greatest quality."

"I have good qualities?" I act astounded.

"You do, though, and that's the problem," she says. "You have such a dour persona, but people do like to be around you. When you allow them, at least."

I mumble an *eh* as I refill the popcorn maker. "I don't buy all of that, but thanks. You're always so nice to me, and I'll never understand why."

"I'm nice to everyone," she affirms. "Deflate your ego."

"That's true," I agree. We share a moment of silence as we look out on the empty theater lobby. The rumble of an occasional car passes outside, but otherwise, the building is completely silent. "Don't you find this depressing?"

"What?" she scoffs. "No crowd? No, I find that kind of relaxing."

"We can't survive without a crowd, Caitlyn."

She knows that the silence is more deafening to me than it could ever be to her, and that is because my future lies with this building's success. So, she tries to make me feel better, once again. "Well, Kylie will be here soon, so we won't have to worry about it being too quiet."

I know she is joking, but somehow that notion does make me feel better. I have grown very fond of my coworkers over the past two years. We have become inseparable both inside and outside of work. Kylie, Caitlyn, and I are all seniors at Harlan High School. Despite our tight friendship, we could not be more different. I can only assume that we would have never interacted with each other if we had not worked together first.

Caitlyn is one of the best people I have ever known. In fact, she may be *the* best. She is kind, smart, and athletic. She is the type of student who every teacher wants to have in class and the type of peer who every teenager wants to have as a friend. She is incredibly driven and already has her whole life planned out. Usually that would be an obnoxious character trait, but with her, it makes sense. And I am happy she has her life so together. She deserves it.

Kylie, on the other hand, is the opposite of Caitlyn in many ways. While Caitlyn stands nearly six feet tall, Kylie barely stands over five feet. More noticeably, though, Kylie does *not* have her life together. When she first started working at the theater as a sophomore, she had brown hair that reached the middle of her back. Now, Kylie has barely-shoulder-length hair that is a light oceanic blue. Kylie likes to joke that she colors and/or cuts her hair with every life crisis she has, but at this point, I do not think she is kidding. She always has drama going on in her life – the type of drama that legitimately makes a person wonder whether some people just don't have a fair shake in life. One would think that the constant drama surrounding Kylie's life would be incredibly annoying, but it really is not. Kylie is always bouncing with energy, singing songs, and dancing to music that only exists in her head. She is the most ridiculous person I have ever met, but she is one of my favorites, too.

  The three of us have two other coworkers – Ronald and Margaret. Yes, they are as old as they sound. Ronnie and Margie are married and have been since the plumbing incident at the Watergate Hotel. They only work Friday and Saturday nights and Sunday afternoons, and they basically do so only out of kindness to my parents. They have been friends with my parents for decades, and they have worked at the theater since the 1980s. It is kind of sweet, in a way. The nostalgic love they have for this place is contagious. I just wish they could rip tickets in half and scoop up popcorn as quickly as they can recite the entirety of last night's episode of *Hannity*.

  "How do you like it?" Kylie asks, bursting through the entrance and silence of the theater. She twirls in place, showing off her new hair. It's now silver with a couple of light streaks of pink.

  "What happened?" I asked.

  "I dyed it, dummy," she replies as she begins to emulate Merton Hanks' famous touchdown dance. I have no idea where she saw the insane dance before – maybe she had not. Maybe it was just instinctual. I only recognize it because I am a devout NFL fan. Caitlyn, however, is clearly not such a fan, as she looks upon Kylie's bobbling dance moves in disgust and horror.

"I know that," I laugh. "I meant, *what happened*? What life crisis took hold of you?"

"Oh," Kylie composes herself as though she were about to be interviewed for a *Vogue* article. "Well, you know how I have been dating that guy from here – Hudson – for two months now?"

"Yeah..." Caitlyn and I answer in unison.

Kylie begins popping and locking and speaking in spurts. "Well – it's – over – now. And thank goodness, right? I didn't want to have to have a celebration for my longest relationship."

"How long was your longest relationship?" Caitlyn asks.

"Two months – and – one week," Kylie responds, starting and, by all accounts, creating an entirely new dance.

I burst out laughing. "I'm sorry. I just don't get it."

"Don't get what?" Kylie stops her routine. She is completely serious.

"I honestly don't get these guys," I respond. "How could you not love you?"

"That was a confusing way to say it, but I totally agree," she answers in a "valley girl" accent. "But, ya know, there are valid reasons, Guy."

"Oh, I'm aware," I say. "The drama overtakes your sense of fun."

"It really does," she laughs. Kylie dances her way behind the counter to join us. "So, what are you guys up to? Busy day?"

"No customers so far today," Caitlyn responds.

"What about last night? You worked, right?"

"It was a smaller crowd than usual, especially for a double. We had a total of thirteen, but only two of them were regulars," Caitlyn says.

"Denny and Craig?" Kylie asks.

"No," Caitlyn responds.

"Ethel and Sandy?"

"No."

"That creepy guy with the Pomeranian who always comes to the animated movies?"

"No," Caitlyn ends the game. "Guy and Bri."

"Oh, that doesn't count," Kylie waves off the information.

"We don't count?" I ask, shocked. "We don't matter?"

"No, not really, in all honesty. None of us do. We are barely evolved amoebas who – still – don't – understand – what – life – is – or – why – we're – here – in – the – first – place!"

"Ugh," Caitlyn growls. "Please stop singing."

"Okay, sorry . . . geez. Didn't realize everyone was gonna be grumpy today. Usually it's just Guy."

"Thanks," I chime.

"Am I wrong?" she asks. "Caitlyn's the good employee, I'm the fun employee, and you're the... well, you're like a supervisor, but without any actual power."

"That's pretty accurate," Caitlyn agrees.

I stand up from the counter and walk away. I think I have finally had enough.

"Sensitive Sally over here," Kylie goads with a thumb as I walk away.

"He's just having a moment," Caitlyn says. "Tough day."

"Why? Did Bri break up with him?"

"No!" I yell from the break room, roughly twenty feet away from the ticket counter. I sit on the old sofa that centers both the room and my mental well-being. "Not yet anyway."

"What's that supposed to mean?" Kylie asks, slowly peaking into the break room, from afar, to look at the sad sack slumped over on the couch.

"He's just being dramatic about . . ."

"The end," I yell.

". . . graduation and the next step."

"Yeah, the next step is to leave me behind," I say, heading to the front of the counter.

"Are you done with your couch time already?" Kylie asks. "Usually you're in there for a good forty-five minutes on bad days."

"I can't have you guys talking about me so loudly and not defend myself."

"We're all graduating," Kylie says, shrugging off my paranoia. "What's the problem? Only Caitlyn has it figured out."

"That's not true," Caitlyn says.

"No, it's kinda true," I agree. "But I'm not like you, Kylie. I need to know what my next step is and, more importantly, that it is *sturdy*. And not gonna leave me."

"That metaphor kinda took a weird turn," Caitlyn says.

"The step is…" I begin.

"The step is Brianna, we get it," Caitlyn fills in. "There's more to life than romance, Guy. Especially one that you created in high school."

"Is there, though?" I say. "That's all you guys ever talk about. I mean, look at Kylie's hair – a result of another failed romance. I do like your hair by the way, Kyle." Caitlyn and I call her Kyle as a form of affection, not ridicule.

"It's okay, you don't have to . . ." Kylie begins.

"No, I'm serious," I say. "Usually I don't like what you do with it, but the silver really pops."

"Oh, well, thank you," Kylie says, swaying back and forth, clasping her hands.

"Focus, you two," Caitlyn says.

"Sorry," we say in unison.

"I get what he's saying a little bit," Kylie agrees with me. It's probably only because I complimented her hair, but I accept the alliance without hesitation. "It's kinda scary not knowing what comes next. Sure, you know what to expect, Caitlyn, because you've been working toward it for four years. Guy and me, though… I think I can speak for both of us when I say we only recently began thinking about this stuff. The next step. And Guy's path is a lot different than ours. Caitlyn, you're going off to college in Oklahoma, and I'm going to New York to waitress and/or bartend and/or strip to save up for my European trip. But Guy… he's staying *here*. That's a real bummer."

The silence that Kylie's entrance shattered now returns. Finally, I break it. "Well, thanks for that, Kylie.

She's right, though. Hopefully not about the stripping thing, but everything else. You guys are leaving this town – and state – to begin new lives while I maintain my exact same life in small town Missouri. How is that not depressing? I'm surprised Brianna didn't just end our relationship when she had the chance last night."

"I thought you said you guys were good?" Caitlyn asks.

"No, we are," I clarify, "I just know…"

"You're impossible, Guy," Caitlyn says as she heads to the breakroom. "The self-pitying is…" Her words dissemble as she exits.

Kylie and I stand in silence, a rarity. I notice the clock on the wall. I love my job here, but time has been crawling lately. I feel suffocated. This building, the place I used to love, has become claustrophobic to me. *Everything I love turns on me.*

"Brianna's not gonna leave you, Guy," Kylie breaks up my in-progress panic attack.

"You really don't think so?"

"I really don't," she says soberly.

"And why is that?"

"Because you're a good guy… *Guy*. You really are. And those are hard to find. Also, you're funny, in a dark and depressing sort of way. And you're tall. Not terribly ugly."

"Thanks, that means a lot," I say and then wait a moment. "Are you just being nice to me because I complimented your hair?"

Kylie looks down and shakes her head. "I meant what I said, but yes. I needed that."

I laugh. "I really meant it. Looks good."

"Thanks," she smiles.

Another pause.

"You really do need a plan, even more than I do," I say to her.

"Yeah, I know," she nods.

"I mean, stripping cannot be an option for you."

"Are you saying I'm ugly? Or that I can't dance?"

"No, that's not what I'm saying. You're a wonderful dancer. I assume your skills would translate to the exotic variety as well. I just mean you're better than that."

"Thanks."

"Plus, if you get destroyed by a two-month relationship, what kind of life do you think you'll have in that line of work?"

"You know what… that is a really good point."

"Thank you."

Another pause.

"But if you *do* disregard my advice…"

"I'll send you the name of the club, no questions asked."

I laugh as I leave the counter and head into the auditorium. *My auditorium.*

3

The Bristol Arts Theater has been struggling to survive since the early 2000s, right around the time I was born. Coincidence? Maybe... *but probably not*. My great grandfather purchased the theater in the early 1940s, during the first run of *Citizen Kane*. Ever since, this building has been the crown jewel in my family's heritage. Well, until semi-recently.

Since the turn of the century, the appreciation for the "theatrical experience" has soured among patrons. Most people would rather stream movies from home on their Roku or Apple TV. After all, most new release movies hit streaming services in less than three months. With all of the entertainment options in the world, that is not too long to have to wait to see the newest superhero movie or Oscar contender.

Since the public is so apathetic about seeing new movies, business has declined everywhere even as individual ticket prices soar. While movies broadcast their "record-breaking numbers," it is actually all a ruse. It is inflation, pure and simple. Fewer people care about the shared movie-going experience, and that is especially true for theaters without IMAX screens, DTS surround sound, or chairs that move with the actions of the film. After sitting in one of those seats for two hours, I didn't know whether to feel violated or to smoke a cigarette in appreciation.

That is exactly what the Bristol Arts Theater is not. While we do have an impressively sized screen, it is not seven stories tall. The 550 seats in the auditorium do not recline or heat themselves. Our staff does not discreetly deliver dinner, ninja-style, to hungry customers. Our theater is an old school theater, designed in 1901, and it has been preserved to remain that way. The only *major* new addition added to its set-up over the past 100 years was a digital projector, which is an absolute requirement to screen modern movies.

And it is all mine. Or soon to be.

You see, my parents had me at an "advanced" age. Since I am an only child, and since my parents conceived me in their fifties, one could safely assume that I was indeed a mistake. That is a heavy burden for a person to carry around all his life.

I have to assume that is why they named me Guy. After enduring a geriatric pregnancy just as they received their AARP cards, I think that "Guy" was simply the best they could do.

"It's a boy? Name it Guy."

It was hard for me to relate to my parents as I grew up. Every family has generational gaps, of course, but our gap was as wide as the Dust Bowl (a bowl in which they, ironically, *were* conceived). I had no one to talk to growing up outside of school, so I quickly made friends with the giants on screen – Humphrey Bogart, Robert DeNiro, Al Pacino, Gene Hackman, and Clint Eastwood. And during my confusing "formative" years, I also fell in love with the women on screen – Diane Keaton, Rita Hayworth, Madeline Kahn, Ingrid Bergman, and Paulette Goddard. Every day after school, I came to the theater and sat through the matinee and sometimes even the evening show. I came here on weekends, arriving early and staying late. I found everything I needed in those films and the people onscreen.

Indulging in so much movie magic did harm my psyche, I must say. Leaving the theater, and the worlds I discovered within it, was always difficult. I would always rather be there than in the real world. My life in Harlan, Missouri, was dull, boring, and lonely. My life inside the Bristol Arts Theater was anything but that. I wanted nothing more than to live there and never leave.

And here I am today, wanting just that – to leave.

Again, my parents were old when they had me, and they have only gotten *exponentially* older over the years. They are both now closing in on seventy, and they both want to retire, or at least step back from their daily responsibilities at the theater. Who could blame them? They have worked their entire lives, and they have done it side-by-side. We all need a break at some point.

So the plan – *their plan* – is this: After I graduate, in approximately five months, I will become the "assistant" manager at the theater, under the co-management of my coworkers, Ronald and Margaret. In actuality, they will be managing in name only. They, too, are knock-knock-knocking on heaven's door, and they see me as their way out as well. While I attend some online classes, via a local community college, to attain the degree I need to run the theater on my own, Ronnie and Margie will act as the face of this dying theater. It is actually kind of poetic.

That is a problem as well, though. This theater is as close to death as are physical film reels (and half of our staff). Our business has plummeted drastically over the past decade. The fact that we are still open at all baffles all other local businesses. Even the guy running the peanut-themed food truck off the town square is shocked. To be fair, though, he may be the smartest businessman in town. No one wants to order a bag of peanuts outside of a baseball game, and yet he is thriving. I think his success all has to do with his marketing. His truck is called "Let's Get Nuts!" and his slogan is "Put My Nuts in Your Mouth." No, I am not kidding.

I did, however, learn a lot from Mr. Peanut. No, nothing involving his nuts, but the way he presented his nuts. *Wait, no*. Well, you get the idea.

To revitalize the Bristol Arts Theater, we had to do something unique to draw people in. We could not afford to completely remodel our theater to rival the busy megaplexes. We had to do something different. That was when I came up with an idea. Well, *two* ideas.

My first idea was simple. People love to drink. Well, most people do anyway. I, myself, do not like alcohol, and as an underage citizen, that is probably the best practice. I do understand that other people enjoy booze, though. Sensing an opportunity, I suggested to my parents that we add on a bar to our concession stand. It did not have to be huge. I suggested we put four types of beer on tap (one heavy domestic, one heavy foreign, one light, and one alternating IPA, or craft beer, for the hipster types trying to impress their dates). I also suggested that we offer a small variety of mixed drinks or cocktails.

Initially, my idea was a huge success. New people started popping into our theater all the time, excited to enjoy a light beer to accompany a similarly light-on-plot movie. Word got out or something, though, because theaters all over the state started to offer alcohol, even chain megaplexes. When that happened, our business dropped further than ever before. That was when I came up with my second idea.

I suggested that we set up monthly double features. We already offered screenings of older films on a weekly basis, and they were honestly the main source of our income, other than Marvel, *Star Wars*, or animated films. The older generations loved to watch classic movies on the big screens again, bringing back the memories and emotions the films elicited decades before. It was a pure nostalgic shot of adrenaline. Because those films were already doing well at our theater, my newest suggestion just built upon that practice.

My idea was simple. I would curate a special double feature every month that thematically paired two films together – one from the "classic" era (pre-1980s) and one from the "modern" era (post-1980). Sometimes we broke the rules a bit (like last night's pairing of *The Wages of Fear* and *Sorcerer* – the latter was released in 1977), but I always tried to adhere to that rule. I wanted to create interest in older films among the younger crowds that only sporadically visited, and I wanted to encourage continued interest in modern films among the steady and reliable older crowd. I viewed it as a win-win scenario all around.

Really, I was correct. The monthly double feature idea took off almost immediately. Just when the Bristol was on the brink of closing, it barely survived. I saved it from its expected death.

Yet I also encouraged my own imprisonment. Because of my "brilliant" idea, I secured my fate, right here in small town, Missouri – *right where I don't want to be*. I know I should be happy that I have created my own job security, but at what cost? How much longer can this theater possibly stay open? Our crowd is getting older and older, and we all know what that means. Once that crowd is gone, I highly doubt younger audiences will suddenly develop a sophisticated taste in cinema. If today's blockbusters are any indicator of where things are headed, we are quickly approaching cinematic doomsday.

Most importantly, everyone I know and care about is leaving. Caitlyn and Kylie are moving to two different states to begin their adult lives. Brianna, my girlfriend whom I truly love, is moving to a *big* city to begin her *big* college life. And my parents...

What about me? It is, by definition, selfish to think about myself, but I cannot help but wonder where my life figures in all of this. Am I supposed to run this barely-surviving theater, essentially on my own, until it closes down in five to ten years? What happens after that? Everyone I know will have already moved on by then. They will have graduated college and/or begun their careers, gotten married, had kids, bought homes, and invested in retirement. In five to ten years, I will have accumulated an impressive movie poster collection and single-handedly curated my parents', surely joint, funeral.

What stands out most, though, is her... *B*. I will have lost her by then. She cannot put her life on hold for me. She is much too… there isn't even a word for what she is. She is funny, smart, quick-witted, outgoing, and sexy. *Man, is she sexy.* She does not even realize her seductive power either, and that's what kills me. She could literally have any man she wanted, and yet she chooses to indulge me. It is truly baffling. The moment she enters the room, she owns it. I can think of nothing other than her presence and how to please her. When we lock eyes, I want to shudder with both satisfaction and dismay because I am not worthy. And when she smiles at me, especially when her head is tilted downward… *forget about it.* I would self-operate and remove one of my own kidneys and sell it on the black market for her. I don't want to get carried away here or anything, but the only thing that is more alluring than her smile is her figure in one of her short, form-fitting outfits. When she wears one of those, whether it is a dress, a romper, or even athletic shorts, my day is done. I am of no use to anyone. I shut down like a laptop doused with water. If Brianna were able to harness her sexual prowess, she could both destroy and save nations.

And she's leaving in five months.

How can I possibly be okay with that? It is just a matter of time before she realizes that Harlan, Missouri, was never the place for her. The people here did not appreciate her for what she was – a transcendent individual. Yes, she is more than good looks. She is the most intriguing person I have ever known, full of depth and emotion and vulnerability. When I talk to her, I want to binge her like a good Netflix show. I seriously can never get enough of her. It will not take long for someone else to realize what a catch she is. And I am sure that guy will be more handsome, funny, and intelligent than this Guy.

These are the things I think about when I am alone in the dark, in the middle of a bunch of empty seats in the Bristol Arts Theater. I get my best thinking done here, but I am struggling to find a peaceful final thought for myself today. The diversion with my coworkers was nice, but that too was fleeting.

It is all about to end.

How can I function alone? Is it possible for me to survive and thrive without anyone around me? Without my loved ones upon whom I currently depend so much?

I look around the near-empty theater for some sort of answer. It is hard to be optimistic, though, with such slim pickings. Tonight, there are five people in here – one couple, two "loners," and myself.

A "loner" is what my coworkers and I call the patrons who attend movies by themselves. They are pretty common, actually, and they are consistent. Growing up, I always thought it was weird to attend movies alone, but as I got older, I understood why people do it. If a person loves film, then he would want to fully immerse himself in the film with as few distractions as possible. So while I was judgmental at first, I came to understand and embrace the "loner" philosophy myself.

That's when I realize something.

There are more than enough people here to help me understand what it is I need to learn – *what I need to embrace.*

I am a loner.

4

As I enter the lobby, I can see that Caitlyn has finished decorating for Christmas. Kylie, meanwhile, has only accomplished making a new playlist on Spotify.

"What do you think?" Caitlyn asks as she proudly shows off the ornamentation as if she were showcasing a speedboat on *The Price is Right*.

"It's looks great, Cate, but I need your help with something," I implore.

"Okay…" she responds hesitantly.

Kylie senses the change in atmosphere and does something she is paid to do but never does – puts her phone in her pocket. Her full attention is also on me.

"I need you to help me find a way to talk to people," I say slowly. "Specifically loners."

Kylie's face morphs in disgust and simply says, "Ew."

"What are you talking about?" Caitlyn says.

"Since Bri is going to be leaving, I need…" I begin.

"Whoa, whoa, whoa," Kylie interrupts, holding up a hand. "You're already chummin' the waters?"

"No," I say firmly. "This isn't about finding a new girlfriend, it's about finding someone to talk to."

Both of my coworkers stare at me blankly.

"And what exactly are we?" Kylie asks defensively. "You're too good to chat us up now? Less than thirty minutes ago you were begging to know what club I was going to strip at."

"What?!" Caitlyn exclaims.

"It's true," Kylie says, arms crossed.

"No, that is not true," I correct.

"Oh, yes, it is," she replies firmly, arms still crossed.

"Well, the stripping thing is probably true, but I was not looking to be her customer," I explain to Caitlyn.

"So, I'm not good enough to talk to and I'm ugly as well? Real nice, Guy," Kylie pouts.

"Stop," Caitlyn says, closing her eyes. "What exactly is going on?"

I take a breath. "I need to figure out how to function on my own. That's what this is all about. That is what I need to learn. In just a few months, everyone is leaving – Bri, Kylie, you. And who knows how many more miles Ronnie and Margie have on their odometers. Not to mention…" I cut myself short.

"I understand why you have anxiety about that, Guy. I really do," Caitlyn says. "But we're not *leaving* leaving you."

"That's what everyone says when they leave town after high school. 'Oh, we'll still hang out, don't worry. We'll send Snaps every day and stay active in the group chat.' But eventually those things go away, too."

My words sink in.

After a moment, Caitlyn says, "What is it you want from me then? What about loners?"

"We see people come to this theater, alone, every day. It's fairly common. Some are weirdos, for sure, but others don't seem so bad. I need to know how they do it. How they can be self-sufficient and seemingly happy and content."

"And you need Caitlyn to run a check on those people first, basically, to see if they're 'okay' people and willing to talk to the gremlin behind the concession stand?" Kylie infers.

"Hey, you just said I wasn't ugly," I remind her.

"That was before you said you didn't want to see me strip," Kylie retorts.

"Fine! I'll come watch you take your clothes off for money! Happy now?" I am exasperated with her future scenario. Kylie is needy in the past, present, and future.

"Well, not if you're going to use that tone," she huffs.

"My tone doesn't matter – it'll be your job," I state matter-of-factly. "I'm sure you'll deal with worse."

"How dare you," she states slowly.

"Can we please stop talking about Kylie's career as a stripper?" Caitlyn shouts. She then turns to Kylie. "While I *firmly* disagree with that choice, if you want to take your clothes off, that's your business." She turns back to me. "And no one is forcing you to throw dollar bills at her ass. Okay?"

"Um…" A timid male customer, about fifteen years old, slowly and shakily holds up his empty popcorn bag to us. He is a loner. "Could I get a refill, please?" he squeaks.

We remain silent in a mixture of horror and suppressed hilarity.

"Yes, right away," Caitlyn says, taking the bag.

The loner awkwardly tries not to stare at Kylie, but he is failing miserably. Kylie playfully gives him a flirtatious smile, pointing her chin to her shoulder and raising her eyebrows, as Caitlyn hands him the filled bag. Once it is in his possession, he scampers off.

Caitlyn stares at Kylie. "You're not going to become an exotic dancer. Okay?"

"Fine," Kylie sniffs.

I cannot help but laugh. "You really are insane," I tell Kylie.

"I know," she smiles.

"Back to you and your equally bizarre scenario, Guy," Caitlyn resumes. "Why me?"

"Yeah," Kylie interjects. "Why her and not me? I'm great at talking to people."

"You are," I hesitantly agree, "but Cate has a certain… sincerity about her."

"I'm not sincere?" Kylie is offended.

"No, you are," I correct. "You're one of the most sincere friends I have. But Cate shows sincerity in a way that appeals to strangers. With you, a person may not know if you're just joking around or being sincere. For instance, take that loner who was just here. Did he believe that bizarre scenario he walked into? Did he think you were actually flirting with him? Is he currently visiting an ATM machine? Sometimes it's hard to tell with you." She is silent. "But that's what makes you great," I resume. "I just need Cate's skillset for this, I think."

"Yeah, you're probably right," Kylie concedes. "Cate is boring like that."

Caitlyn ignores the comment. "Which loners should I target?" she asks.

"I'm not sure that's the terminology I'm looking for," I say.

"Okay," she corrects. "What kind of people should I be on the lookout for? People who look like you?"

Kylie chuckles. "I don't think a lot of sad, lonely looking males attend the movies alone. No, wait…"

I, too, ignore her comment. "No, the exact opposite. I know what I'm like. I could probably easily relate to another guy who is afraid of losing his girlfriend, not having a stable job, losing his friends, and being stuck in his hometown forever. No, I need to relate to people who are seemingly much different than me. I need to find that universal truth that relates to hopelessness."

"Wow," Caitlyn says. "No pressure."

"Sorry, that does seem like a lot," I admit. "Kylie, you can help in this process, too. I'm sure you would be great at evaluating others by their looks. Handing out judgements based on no evidence."

"I know you meant that as an insult," Kylie says, "but I am on it. No – one – judges – others – quite – like – me," she sings.

"This is good," I say with certainty. "Just don't mention it to Brianna, okay?"

"I won't," Caitlyn agrees. "After all, you're not doing anything wrong."

"Thank you," I agree. "Kylie?"

Kylie looks down at her phone. "It's okay, she hasn't opened the message yet."

"Kylie!"

"I'm just kidding," she says, waving a nonchalant hand at me. "Have I ever betrayed your trust before?"

I choose to ignore the countless times in which she has. "Thanks," I mumble.

"When does our little operation begin?" Kylie asks, rubbing her hands together slowly as if she were rolling up a Play-Doh snake.

"It needs to be on nights that we all work together," I think out loud.

"Weekends," Caitlyn agrees.

"And ideally, it needs to be when we have a substantial shift together, so that we can work everything out. Like nights when we spend hours together."

"Like today," Caitlyn acknowledges.

"Exactly."

"How about we do it on our double feature nights?" Kylie suggests.

"That's great!" I confirm. "We have like five more of them before…" I suddenly trail off. I am so caught up in the excitement of the moment – planning out an engaging scenario with my friends – that I almost forget the reason behind it all.

Caitlyn picks up on my hesitation. "Double-feature nights. Sounds fun," she smiles.

"Five weeks to figure out how Guy can find happiness in a life of certain solitude," Kylie smirks and throws an arm around me. "Sounds easy enough."

PART TWO

THE GRADUATE

SILVER LININGS PLAYBOOK

5

January's weather intensifies and solidifies what is already in my headspace. The cold, dry wind that wants to shatter your bones the moment you leave the comfort of your home... the hard, unforgiving ground that pushes against every step you take in progression... the white, barren horizon that seems to offer no sign of forgiveness or escape...

How people can actually celebrate a new year in the midst of this horrendous month is truly mind-boggling. *What is there to celebrate?* New Year's should be celebrated in May – when life seems to be full and exciting and warm. In January, there is no disguising the truth – life is painful, dreary, and lonely.

I think about January as I walk. I also think about how I am making a mistake with Brianna as well. *I am pushing her away*. I am aware of my actions, and that is what is so infuriating. She has shown me nothing but love in our relationship. She has never wavered in that. Never once did I hear about the usual high school relationship drama that seems to plague *every. single. couple.*

I never heard from my friends that she was texting other guys or sending flirty photos. She never gave a male classmate a ride home in her car "even though it was out of her way," and she never took such a ride either. After all, let's be real – we all know what those rides are about. The close confines that enable impassioned, previously pent-up feelings. The quiet conversations that no one else ever has to know about. The hands that, according to all future accounts, never actually crossed over the gear shift. The *need* to pull over to the side of the road. We all know that those "innocent" rides given to classmates are a ruse.

She never did any of that. She simply *loved* me. She gave me all of her attention and affection, without being overbearing or obnoxious. Not that she could ever be overbearing with me. If she wanted to have a surgery that merged our two bodies like two conjoined twins, I would sign the waiver in a shared heartbeat. I love her more than she could ever love me.

So why am I such an idiot when it comes to our relationship?

It is because sabotage is easier to manage. If I push Bri away now, it will be easier for me. Later on, in just a few months, I will be forced to let her go. That is the worst kind of heartbreak – the slow, drawn-out kind. I do not want Old Yeller to die, but I know the Lord is gonna take him before too long, so I may as well cap him off now. Quick and easy. You get what I mean.

What it comes down to is this – I would rather give Brianna up than have her taken away.

Brianna, however, is oblivious to my current mindset, as sound as it seems to be to me. To her, this whole post-high school/college turmoil is nothing. "It'll all work out," she constantly says, "because we are in love." It is a nice, hopeful thought, but I am a realist. As I just learned in history class, Nixon defeated McGovern, and distance will defeat our relationship.

As a near high school graduate, I see the whole thing as a simple equation: $D = TA = NO = P$. In other words, *Distance = Time Away = New Opportunities = Problems.*

Look, as I mentioned, I am not an overbearing man, or at least I try not to be. I want B to have her independence – to experience all aspects of life, even those that do not involve me (just preferably not the ones that involve other dudes).

Distance, however, will always be a problem. I will not be minutes away when she needs me in a crisis or when she is feeling down. She will have to find that kind of solace elsewhere. FaceTime does not suffice in such crises. A person needs real, physical contact in scenarios like that. A comforting pat on the back... a warm hug... a friendly kiss on the cheek... a caring notice that her hair is covering her pained face... a careful tucking of a strand behind her ear that leads to more caressing of her long, silky hair... running his fingers down lower and lower as she looks up at him with soft, yet hurt, eyes... *Ugh.*

Distance = Time Away.

In that time away from each other, she will inevitably meet a bunch of new people at college, and that is great. It really is. I, however, stuck here between my home in Harlan and the theater in Hudson, will not have those same opportunities. So while I am living my same old life, she will be experiencing a whole new, exciting life – one that she was never able to experience in small town Missouri. How is that not a positive? She can, and must, take advantage of those new opportunities.

Time Away = New Opportunities.

What is left after that? After she experiences a big city full of diverse, interesting, smart, and driven people from all walks of life? Quite simply ... Problems. All of a sudden, the unique "kid" from Harlan who loved movies, music, and books is not so unique anymore. And that is exactly what he seems like now – a *kid*. In her college town, her classmates will be arguing about the futility of two-party political systems, visiting art museums, taking road trips to attend concerts, and having late-night rap sessions where the "woke" dudes discuss the origins of the universe (and, presumably, the ultimate demise of it), while passing around a joint and listening to John Coltrane on vinyl.

If you really listen, man, to the trombone, like follow it all the way through the song, and even more importantly the album as a whole, it transports you to the studio in that moment in time, and you can feel the tension between the musicians, the generous give and selfish take that each of them undertakes while performing as a band while also wanting to shine as individual artists, and that's when – and only when – you can understand it, man . . . you understand what this is all about . . . the music is us, and the vibe of the intertwining instruments is the intertwining of us as people, of us as nations, and how we want to come together, but our desire to outshine each other will always rule . . . after all, man, the album is John Coltrane's – not the band's . . . he took ownership, and that is what it is all about . . . that's how you can make sense of it all, and how life can become equal parts calming and anxiety-ridden . . . the give-and-take, man.

How can I possibly compete with that sort of enlightenment?

New Opportunities = Problems.

Another problem is Brianna herself. She is such an interesting person, full of energy and a compelling life force. I am not a user of drugs or alcohol, but I imagine that she is what junkies chase after every night. Junkies spend their whole day, from the moment they wake up, ready to find that fix – that *high*. They sell out family members, abuse the kindness of strangers, and degrade themselves for a measly twenty-dollar hit that comes in a grimy plastic bag that is smaller than your thumb. But when that hit comes at 10 o'clock at night, it is all worth it. And it will be equally worth it the next morning when they wake up completely sober and ready to chase that dragon again.

That is how I feel about Brianna. Luckily, she is not a harmful drug that can end my life, but the sensation of being around her is a *high*. I love it. I love to just watch her do the normal, everyday things – put on her shoes, start her car, talk to her friends, casually brush her hair out of her eyes, watching her after a conversation ends and she is just in her head for a moment. She is beautiful in the most unassuming way. I know that sounds stalker-ish, but it's really not. I like watching her in her element because I envy God in those moments. Man, how He must have felt when He created her. *Perfection*. Luckily, God did not hang it up after her creation like Peyton Manning did after winning his last Super Bowl. In all honesty, though, I am not sure He will ever top her. No, Brianna is not perfect, no human is, but her faults are nearly completely diminished by her incredible attributes.

To top it all off, Brianna is drop-dead gorgeous. Sure, I am in danger when it comes to other guys the moment she has a conversation with any given one of them. As soon as she shows her individuality, it would be hard for anyone not to fall in love with her. When you combine that personality with her looks . . . "I'm in danger," as Ralph Wiggum would say. Somehow, she looks both exotic and "girl next door." She has dark brown hair that flows just past her shoulders and dark, smokey eyes to match. *Don't even get me started on her eyes* . . . She has olive-colored skin and an athlete's body. Most importantly, though, her body fits into mine perfectly when we embrace. Her arms wrap around my waist and the top of her head just reaches the bottom of my chin. It's like connecting two Legos, with that satisfying "snap" that occurs with placement. It is as if God, in all of his generosity, suited us for each other in every way possible.

Except for our future paths.

And that is what happens every time I think about the good things in my life – I am reminded of the impending gloom.

The shit month of January.

But there is hope. I am not walking in the harsh weather today as a form of self-flagellation. Instead, I am walking because I am prepping for my first "loner experience."

6

"Well your mama kept you but your daddy left you
And I should've done just the same
But I came to love you
Am I gonna bleed?
Oh, oh, oh, I got a love that keeps me waiting
I'm a lonely boy"

Kylie dedicates a special song for me on her Bluetooth speaker as I enter the theater.

"Thanks, Kylie," I muster as I take off my coat and hat.

"It's 'Lonely Boy' by The Black Keys," she states proudly.

"I know the song," I respond firmly. I look around. "Where's Cate?"

"She's upstairs, she'll be right back," she answers. She looks me over for a second, overjoyed. "So are you ready for your big 'loner' experience today? I'm so proud of you, opening up to others."

"Shut up," I say like a child. "It may not even happen. Everything needs to play out perfectly. First off, we need loners to show up." I nod my head toward the screening room. "How's the crowd today so far?"

"Pretty slim," she admits, "but more will come for the double feature."

"You think?" I ask, looking for reassurance. "Even in this weather?"

"I mean, I don't like the old movies, but other people seem to," she shrugs.

Tonight's double feature is sure to be a hit, by all accounts. First, we are screening Mike Nichols' 1967 classic *The Graduate*, followed by David O. Russell's 2012 modern classic *Silver Linings Playbook*. Just like every other month, I chose the line-up of the two films weeks in advance. Mom and Dad are more than happy to turn over every possible responsibility to me when they can.

I look at the clock on the wall. "I guess we'll find out in thirty minutes."

Six o'clock, the start-time for the first film, quickly arrives amidst my nervousness. Caitlyn and Kylie, both on ardent friend duty, have been double-manning the register to scope out all potential loners, and there are plenty to choose from tonight. Roughly sixty people appear to be in attendance tonight, and while that may seem small for a house that seats more than five hundred, that is a big movie night for us. Enormous. The only time the Bristol Arts Theater gets even larger crowds than tonight is when we are booked by a school play, a child beauty pageant, or a funeral.

"What do you think?" I ask the girls hesitantly as the last customer leaves the concession stand line. "Do I have any options tonight?"

"You have plenty of loner options," Caitlyn acknowledges, "but which one is the *right* choice? We probably only have one shot at this. Otherwise, we will look like religious fanatics peddling literature or something."

"She's right," Kylie confirms. She has taken on the persona of a military general overlooking a battlefield moments before action. She stares off into the distance. "We only have one shot at this."

"Did you see anyone that looked suitable?" Caitlyn asks her.

"Well, if we are looking for loners who are the opposite of Guy, there did seem to be a couple," Kylie says. "First off, I think we need to choose a woman. That seems a fitting opposite for Guy, not so much in personality but in body shape."

"Thanks," I shake my head. "Gender-shame me some more, please."

"Oh shut up," Kylie waves me off. "Sensitive Sally. No, it should be a woman because of what you said before – you need to connect with someone similar but completely different, and I think choosing a woman to talk to is the best way to fully initiate yourself in this process."

"You're really taking this seriously, aren't you?" Caitlyn seems proud.

"I am," she agrees. "I think I have a future in judging people. Anyway, we have a few female loner options. Do you have any input about what type of woman it should be?" she asks me. "Older or somewhat your age? You can't be completely uncomfortable if you're going to talk to a total stranger."

I ponder the option quietly. I guess I take too long.

"Come on, who are you more comfortable talking to? Your grandma or a cousin?" Kylie insists.

"A cousin, I guess," I answer with a snap.

"Okay, good," she nods. "I think I have the perfect loner for you then."

I breathe a sigh of relief. "Good. So you just tell Caitlyn which one it is, during the intermission, and then Caitlyn will approach the female loner before the second movie starts."

"It kind of sounds like we are planning a kidnapping or something," Caitlyn says uneasily. "Like Buffalo Bill tricking that lady into moving that couch into his van."

"I know," I agree, "but if you do all the talking, Cate, with your supreme kindness and charm, I really think this will work."

Caitlyn shrugs. "It's worth a shot."

I smile. *What a weird life I live.* "What are we going to do in the meantime? We have about an hour and forty until intermission."

"Roof?" Kylie suggests.

"What about the concession stand? And the door?" Caitlyn reminds us.

Right on cue, Ronnie and Margie enter the Bristol.

"Hey, guys!" Kylie greets. "We were just talking about you."

"All lies, I'm sure," Ronnie teases with a laugh that soon turns into a violent coughing fit. We all hold our breath as if our collective effort will help fill his impaired lungs. Finally, he composes himself.

"We would never tell stories about you, Ronnie," Kylie says as though she were a grandchild buttering up her grandfather for birthday money on her one annual visit to the nursing home. Say what you will about Kylie's work ethic, but there is something to the art of people-pleasing. While she may not be a great worker in the "traditional" sense, she is an artist when it comes to interacting with others, no matter the type of person.

"What did you need, hon?" Margie asks in sweet eagerness.

"We were just wondering if you could man the register for a while so that we could go upstairs and study for a chemistry test together?" Kylie asks, swaying ever so slightly. "It's our first big test of the semester."

"Of course, you three go do what you need to do," Margie says, shuffling us off. "That's why Ronnie and I are here!"

"Thank you," the three of us say in unison.

"Just don't be gettin' up to any hanky panky up there," Ronnie waves a finger. "Guy knows what I am talkin' about!"

With that, Ronnie endures another life-threating laugh/coughing fit, as well as a scolding from Margie.

7

Caitlyn, Kylie, and I love going to the roof. Even in the worst cold or heat, there is something very communal about sharing an illegally accessed spot, like a rooftop, with friends. There is nothing quite like it. Of course, we never mention to Ronnie and Margie that we actually go upstairs, via the left staircase, and outside onto a balcony that sticks out from the side of the building. We then pull ourselves up from the balcony and onto the top of the building. No, they would fear for our safety, but we also figure that 'ol Ron and Marge conducted more than their own share of shenanigans during their day as well.

I help push Kylie up to the roof, I pull myself up next, and then I help pull Caitlyn up last. I probably do not even need to assist Caitlyn – she is by far the most athletic of our trio – but I guess I do for a sense of chivalry. Once we are all up, we assume our usual places. We already have three camping chairs stashed up here, but Kylie usually forgoes her chair and lies down instead. Tonight is no different.

Once we arrive at our positions, we conduct our various rituals. I pull out a Red Bull that I always have safely secured in my coat; Caitlyn pulls out her phone and finds a suitable playlist; and Kylie pulls out her Bluetooth speaker and sets it in the middle of our circle.

"What's it going to be tonight, Cate?" Kylie asks.

"What are you in the mood for?" Caitlyn asks back, scrolling through her phone.

Kylie considers. "Something trippy."

"Oh, no," Caitlyn and I both say.

With that, Kylie pulls a joint from her pocket. "What?"

"Why do you always have to do that?" I ask.

"I don't *always*," she says, searching her pockets for a lighter.

"More often than not," Caitlyn agrees.

"It calms me," Kylie says through her obstructed mouth. She flicks the lighter and stares at us, gauging our expressions. Kylie knows that we are not prudes or anything, but as a duo, we discourage the use of drugs, especially for people as emotionally unbalanced as Kylie. She lets the fire burn for a minute, staring at us through the flame. Then, she releases her thumb from the lighter, extinguishing the flame. "Fine, I won't tonight, but I will next time. You guys need to loosen up."

"Thank you," Caitlyn and I both say, sighing gratefully.

Kylie stares at us, waiting for instruction. "Well, if you're gonna ruin my fun, you better have a good back-up plan."

I scratch my neck as I look down at the roof. "How about handball?"

Caitlyn cheers on the idea while Kylie groans.

"Of course, you guys want to play that *again*," Kylie complains. "Guy invented the game and Caitlyn is a born champion."

She is right on both accounts. I invented the game, or at least my version of it, a couple years ago while wasting time between screenings. The idea behind the game is pretty simple. It can be set up as a game of duos or one-on-one, and essentially it follows the basic rules of tennis or, more appropriately maybe, ping pong. The handball "court" is roughly eight feet by twelve feet. We used Duct tape on the Bristol's roof to make sure the court stays "legal." To play, the server takes the handball, which is dodgeball-esque ball with a seven inch diameter, and bounces it once before serving it to the other side. Once the ball is over the line, the other player(s) must return the serve after the it hits the ground one time. And on and on it goes. If you hit outside the court's lines or don't get out of the way of a bad volley, then the opposing side gets a point. The first team to get to eleven points wins. I realize it sounds like a simple playground game or something, but I assure you it is not. It brings out the extreme competitiveness (and anger) in all of us. It is a game of champions.

    And that is why Kylie hates it, of course. Despite her slender and athletic build, she is anything but athletic. She has only gone out for one sport in her life – track. As a freshman, she joined the team to try to push herself to her limits for a change, but the effort did not last long. During the stretches of the first practice, the track coach – an older gentleman who wore a bucket hat and grimace every day to practice – came over and looked down on her with disgust. He was a man of few words, but he found a couple that day. He told her, "Kylie, you have the flexibility of a dead cow." After that, she quit the team.

    "Do we even have any more balls up here?" Caitlyn asks, looking around.

    "They're probably all down in the street," Kylie mumbles. "Guy can't handle losing and always hits it too hard when he falls behind."

"Well, that doesn't happen too much, Kylie," I sneer, "because I never lose."

"Umm," Caitlyn says, holding up a finger, "I don't believe that's true."

"Those didn't count," I argue. "Those were exhibition matches and you know it." Caitlyn and Kylie both groan and I throw up my hands and yell "What?" over and over. Finally, I spot a ball, tucked behind our cooler. "Got one. Let's do it. Who's first?"

Kylie immediately steps back as Caitlyn steps onto the court and falls into her trademark stance. I will admit it… she intimidates me. "Let's ball," she says with her right arm held back into the air, ready to return my serve.

Caitlyn and I go back and forth in a close game. Kylie keeps score and acts as our line judge. Despite how great she is at people judging, she is actually quite terrible at handball judging. Her calls are terrible for both sides, though, so we allow it. It is part of what makes the game so invigorating.

Before I know it, the score is nine to ten in Caitlyn's favor.

"Game point," Kylie calls out loudly, just to irritate me.

"I know!" I shout. "Just serve it."

Caitlyn sends one over with just the right amount of spin. The bounce nearly takes me off balance, but I fall to the rooftop and return the volley to tie the game. As I get up to my feet, I cannot help but wonder what Ronnie and Margie think is happening during our homework session. Ronnie is probably all smiles. After all, he called it earlier – "Guy knows what I'm talking about."

"Game point," Kylie calls out again.

"No!" I turn and shout at her. "You have to win by two!"

"Alright, geez, this isn't an Olympic sport, Guy," she mutters. "Guy's serve."

I stare Caitlyn in the eyes, trying to figure out the perfect serve to bring her down. Finally, I got it. I am going to side-hand it and put some extra stank on it. My hope is that she cannot move out of the way fast enough and the ball will hit her feet, giving me the point.

I serve up the stank, but it is a close call.

"Over the line," Kylie says. "Caitlyn's point."

"What?" I scream. "That clearly hit her feet!"

Caitlyn just smiles as she picks up the ball. She knows it is a bad call, too.

"I'm the judge, am I not?" Kylie shoots back.

I groan.

"Caitlyn's serve."

Caitlyn does not take the time to evaluate the perfect serve as I did, because she does not need to. She is a born champion. As the ball crosses to my side, I return it with force and precision. It hits within her side of the court, but the ball swiftly takes another bad bounce and leaves the roof.

"You just couldn't handle it, could you?" Kylie says, shaking her head.

"What are you talking about?" I spit out. "That was a legit accident. And my point, might I add."

"You have a real problem with women, don't you?" Kylie shakes her head some more.

"Are you serious right now?"

"You think you're sooo superior…"

"You don't know what you're talking about. I love women."

"Women? *Women*? *Plural*? I'll be sure to tell Brianna that."

"Oh, just stop it."

Caitlyn steps up between us and laughs. "Guy doesn't have a problem with women…"

"Thank you," I add.

"…he just has a problem with losing."

I hesitate. "That's… actually, that's pretty accurate."

I hug it out with Caitlyn as Kylie says, "Can we just sit down and enjoy ourselves now?"

We find our seats around the circle. I take a swig from my Red Bull can and wipe the sweat from my brow as the girls both check their phones.

"Is it sexist to say that girls check their phones more quickly than guys do?" I ask.

"Actually, that *is* sexist, Guy," Caitlyn says, not looking up.

"Sorry, just thought I'd ask." I take another swig. "*Sexist but accurate*," I mumble through the can.

"If you must know, *Guy*, I have to keep track of my new followers," Kylie asserts.

"Followers on what?" I ask. "Instagram, Tik Tok, or Snapchat?"

"All of them," she says, "but mostly the first two. I give out prizes when I hit five hundred new followers for each of those."

"Are you serious?"

Kylie drops her phone. She is completely bewildered and, somewhat, hurt. "Don't you follow my accounts?"

"Well, yeah, I mean, I do, but, uh… no, I mean, I don't get on very much, so…"

Kylie shakes her head. "Some friend."

"What kinds of prizes do you give out?" I ask.

"I'll record a new dance or go live when I hit five hundred. If I hit a thousand, then I send out personal messages, via my personal Snapchat, for anyone who Venmos me at least one dollar. It's a huge discount."

I am both confused and scared. "Well, how much does it usually take for you to send out personal messages like that?"

"Usually fifty dollars."

"Fifty dollars?!" I shout as Caitlyn looks up from her phone as well. "Kylie, I want to be honest with you… that sounds kinda…"

"Shady," Caitlyn says.

"Yeah," I say with actual concern. "That seems like a bad idea. I mean, have you ever watched any of the true crime documentaries on Netflix?"

"It's not like that, guys," Kylie says, rolling her eyes. "I'm only seventeen. I don't do stuff like that. I just, ya know… take requests. Simple ones."

Caitlyn and I both stare. "What would be a simple request?" I ask.

Kylie tilts her head to think. "Like I'll send a Snap of me taking off my shoes and then do close-ups on my feet. Bend my toes, rub my feet together… that kind of thing."

Caitlyn and I are now both slack-jawed. "Who the hell requests that? Quentin Tarantino?"

"You'd be surprised, Guy."

After that, I shut down. I feel as though I have traveled down a darkened path I did not want to venture down. I look over at Caitlyn for some kind of solace. "What are you doing over there?" I ask. "Hopefully not teasing serial killers."

"No, I was actually checking my student email – my college email."

"You already have a student account set up?" Kylie asks.

"Yeah, and they just sent out notices about roommates."

"Oh, that's exciting," Kylie says as if she has forgotten that she is a part of some weird internet fetish on the dark web. "Who is your roomie gonna be?"

"I don't know her," Caitlyn responds, "but she is going to be on the school's basketball team like I am. That's probably why we're rooming together. It says she's from here, though – Hudson."

"You should hang out before you move in together, don't you think?" Kylie says.

"Yeah, maybe," Caitlyn says somewhat hesitantly. "What do you think, Guy? Think that's a good idea?"

"Yeah, maybe," I echo back. Silence looms as both girls stare back at me. "What?"

"Oh, that was just *soo* insightful, Guy," Kylie says.

"What?" I parrot again. I suddenly have the conversation abilities of an Italian grandfather being interrogated by police for shady activities he committed decades ago.

"I just think it's interesting that you have no problem telling me what I should do with my life, but when Caitlyn asks for some input, you dummy up," Kylie says. "I mean, we're all friends here. You should be open with all of us."

I look at Caitlyn and shrug. It is all I can manage.

"It's okay," she tells me. "I understand."

"What do you understand?" Kylie asks defensively.

"He just doesn't want to think about that," she replies.

"What? College?" Kylie asks me. I shrug in response. "You gotta get over that, Guy. I am not trying to be mean, but these things are going to happen, whether you're ready for them or not."

I exhale a loud breath. "You still have that joint?"

Kylie promptly pulls it out. "Wanna spark it up, bro?"

I laugh. "No, I'm just teasing." I turn to face Caitlyn. "I'm sorry. She's right, though. I do need to get over this…"

"Fear," Caitlyn finishes. "That's all it is. You can get over that."

"Yeah, but how?" I mumble. It is not even a question. It is more of a state of mind.

"No matter what it is, you get over your fear by doing – doing what it is you're afraid of."

"I guess a lot of people in Hudson are afraid of sheep," Kylie thinks aloud.

Caitlyn and I both crack up. A moment of happiness reminds me how fleeting everything is, and so I check the time on my phone. Caitlyn notices.

"Is it time?" she asks.

"Just about," I say as I stand up from my chair. Kylie and Caitlyn follow suit.

We walk back over to the side of the roof and climb back down onto the balcony. As we make our way back downstairs to the lobby to help out Ronnie and Margie, I cannot help but think how much I will miss studying for chemistry tests.

8

The three of us return to the lobby and spot Ronnie and Margie. They have stationed themselves on the opposing staircase (two dual ones lead to the upstairs area), as is their norm. They always sit on the lower steps while the movies run, each quietly reading a book. There is something sweet about their ritual. Sharing a moment with each other, even at their advanced ages, without even communicating directly with each other.

"Intermission time already?" Margie asks, slowly rising. Ronnie finishes his paragraph and then places a bookmark in his Lee Child novel. I bend my neck to see that Margie has been re-reading *Born to Run* by Bruce Springsteen. This should come as a surprise to no one, as we all know that Margie has had the biggest crush on the Boss for decades now.

"Just about," Caitlyn acknowledges.

As Ronnie and Margie walk behind the concession stand, the three of us huddle at the bottom of our staircase.

"Okay, so here's the plan," Kylie begins. "Caitlyn is going to approach the loner that I have already picked out. The scenario that Guy presented to us is super creeps, so here's what you're gonna say, Cate… You're going to say that Guy is prepping a college application essay, and he needs to interview a recent college grad so that he has a better understanding of what to expect his first year out of high school."

"Okay," Caitlyn nods, taking in all the directions as if it were a life or death operation.

"That way, it gives Guy a non-threatening way to begin a convo with this lady, and then he'll be good to go," Kylie finishes. "And really, it's not far from the truth. You do need that kind of knowledge from a recent college student – someone who is officially a part of the 'real' world."

"I suppose that's right," I admit.

"You're damn right it is," Kylie points a finger at me. "Don't question me."

"Yes, ma'am," I say with a proud smile.

"You good to go, Guy?" Kylie asks. "Cate?"

We nod in unison.

"We're live in three, two…"

A majority of the patrons simultaneously exit the two sets of auditorium doors. A double feature is nearly impossible to endure without a restroom break, not to mention a replenishing of snacks. Once the outburst of people occurs, Kylie scans the crowd for her loner. After the doors stop swinging, she looks worried.

"She's not out here," she says.

"She's probably just waiting out the crowd," Caitlyn says. "Why don't you go in there and see if you can spot her? The house lights are up."

Kylie agrees and walks through the nearest set of doors. Caitlyn and I hang back and patiently wait for her return. We do not even think of our job duties during this operation, which is kind of cruel to Ronnie and Margie, but they are pros. They can handle scoopin' corn and refillin' Coke just fine. After roughly two long minutes, Kylie returns.

"She's on the left side of left side of the auditorium – third section, roughly two thirds of the way back," she alerts us.

The Bristol Arts Theater has seating set up in three sections. The middle section is the widest, but it is straddled by smaller sections on either side, and apparently this loner is on that left side.

"Okay," Caitlyn nods. "What does she look like?"

"Very pretty," Kylie begins, "with a mixture of confidence and coyness. Like she knows she could land any man she wanted, but she is not that aggressive in her tactics. Or maybe she is… maybe that's how she plays it. Girl next door meets seductress."

"Okay, let's focus more on looks," Caitlyn replies, "as opposed to her dating technique."

"Right," Kylie nods. "She is a brunette – possibly dark red, though. Slender build and tall. She has legs for days. She dresses really pretty. Like casual, but expensive casual. She has small, yet defined, eyebrows and, possibly, deep green eyes. It was kind of hard to tell from far away. She isn't wearing much – if any – makeup, because she, frankly, doesn't need it. She has natural beauty. That is where her power lies. And while slim, she has a booty on her, and her upstairs ain't too shabby either." She pauses to think. "Does that give you a good enough idea?"

"Yeah, I think I got the picture," Caitlyn chuckles. "I feel like I need to clear my search history every time I talk to you."

"Good," Kylie smiles deviously. "Let's do this thing."

With that, Caitlyn walks into the auditorium. The two doors she walks through swing back and forth ever so slightly after her exit, like saloon doors, which is kind of appropriate. What I am about to undertake is a showdown of sorts.

Only it's my future happiness that lies in the balance.

9

"She's in!" Caitlyn exclaims, bursting back through the doors.

"Just like that?" I ask in bewilderment.

"Just like that," she shrugs.

"What did you tell her?" I ask. "The college essay thing?"

"Yes," Caitlyn nods, "and she seemed totally down with helping an incoming student."

"I'm such a genius," Kylie gloats. "It's about time you guys acknowledge my excellence."

"I'm a believer after this," I admit. "So when do I go in for the talk?"

"She said you could watch the second feature with her, if you'd like," Caitlyn says. "After that, she will be more than willing to help you."

"Watch the movie with her?" I shriek. "I wasn't looking for a blind date!"

"It's not a date, you moron," she affirms. "She's just friendly. Not every encounter with the opposite sex leads to… well, sex. You have to be more open-minded, Guy. You need to be chill."

"You're right," I nod. "I can do this."

"So go do it," Kylie says, pushing me.

And I do.

"Hi," I stammer like some middle-school moron approaching a girl for a slow dance at Homecoming. "My coworker just talked to you, I believe."

"Guy, right?" the woman says. "The soon-to-be-high-school grad?"

"That's right," I confirm and then pause. "I'm sorry, my friend didn't tell me your name."

"Here, sit down," she says, holding down the springed-seat next to her. "My name is Maya. I'll be glad to help you out with your essay."

"Great, thank you so much," I say. Suddenly, my whole body begins to uncontrollably shake in nervousness. I am reminded of Katharine Hepburn. *Chill out, Guy!* "It really means a lot to me. I don't want to ask too much of you or… seem like a weirdo or something."

Maya laughs. "I don't think you're a weirdo, at least not yet." She pauses. "This isn't some weird pick-up scenario, right?"

"A-a-absolutely not," I stammer, still waiting for my opportune moment for that slow dance.

"You're just a nervous high schooler, worried about the 'adult world'?"

"One hundred percent correct," I acknowledge with a chuckle. "Especially the nervous part."

"Alright, nothin' wrong with that," she says as the house lights in the theater dim. "Why don't we watch this next movie and then I'll help you out with whatever you need. Sound good?"

"Sounds great," I agree.

"Have you seen this one?" she asks.

"*Silver Linings Playbook*? Many times. It's one of my favorites."

"Perfect, just don't spoil anything for me, okay?" she insists. "I haven't seen it yet, and I hate movie-talkers. You're not a movie-talker, are you, Mr. Jitters?"

"Absolutely not," I say with certainty.

"Good," she smiles. "It's nice to meet you, Guy." She whispers, holding out her hand.

At that moment, the opening titles appear onscreen.

10

Watching a movie next to someone – *anyone* – is often a weird experience. I do not fully engage with the cinematic experience if I am not solo. I do not give my full laugh at comedic scenes, I do not shift in my seat during suspenseful scenes, and I sure as shit do not cry at emotional scenes. I only made that mistake one time.

I recently watched the Mr. Rogers documentary, *Won't You Be My Neighbor*, and I faced a rare occurrence of silent public weeping. It happened during the scene in which Mr. Rogers held a sing-a-long with a terminally-ill child. I could not hold back, and yet I needed to, because I was sitting next to a roided-out skinhead covered in tattoos. That theater may as well have been the animal kingdom. I could not show weakness. The alpha lion would sniff out Mr. Sensitive Lion and rip out his throat so that he had no weak competition to challenge his mating. *Story of my life*. But Mr. Rogers… I could not contain myself. During that heartfelt scene, I cried more than I ever had in public. I put my head in the crook of my arm and silently wept male tears. You know the type. The male cry consists of one or two loud exhales, followed by shoulder shudders and two loud sniffs. It is finished off by a quick wiping of the eyes and an "Oh, geez" as if the cry were some sort of bizarre occurrence, like a comet that only streaks across the skies once every forty years. To any onlookers, I probably looked as though I was having some sort of seizure. Once the movie was over, I bolted out of the theater. I ran from the scene of shame. Right when I stepped outside, though, I heard, "Hey, you!"

I turned around and spotted the alpha lion beckoning me. "Yes?" I whimpered, slowly presenting my vulnerable throat.

"Sad movie, huh?" he asked as he walked up to me. His gait was the most masculine thing I had ever seen. Like John Wayne hopping off a steed to roll up a cigarette and strike a match off his boot.

"Yeah, it had its moments," I reluctantly agreed.

"I wrote to Mr. Rogers when I was a kid," he said. "I never expected him to reply, but he did. He sent me a handwritten response. I'll never forget that. He was a good man."

With that, the alpha turned away to return to his pride. I stared, bewildered. I learned a valuable lesson that day. I am not sure exactly what it was – I'm not as smart or precise as Mr. Rogers was – but there was a lesson learned. Something about book covers, probably.

Luckily, Maya is not as intimidating as that walking tattoo was, but she is still intimidating in her own way. First off, she is a woman. That may not seem fair to say, but it is true, especially from the perspective of a high-school male. I am one hundred percent committed to my relationship with Brianna, but attractive women always make men uneasy. It's science. It's biology. It's *anatomy*.

Maya seems to be enjoying the movie, though. She laughs at the proper times and leans forward interested at pique moments as well. She is a good moviegoer, I can tell. So while my body is falling into rigor mortis, trying to keep my elbow off the armrest and my leg from grazing hers, Maya is fully immersed in the experience.

And just like that, the movie ends. People begin to stand as David O. Russell's name appears onscreen. They shuffle out as Maya and I remain seated.

It is time for the experiment to begin.

"From what your coworker told me, albeit briefly and a tad frantically, you are the employee who chooses two films to pair for these double features. Is that correct?" Maya asks.

"Yeah, that's right," I answer. "It's my favorite thing to do here."

"Why did you pair these two films together?" Maya positions herself in her chair to face me. "*The Graduate* and *Silver Linings Playbook?*"

I turn it over in my head. "Well, obviously there's a sort of 'unhealthy' romance thing going on in both of them. The age difference in *The Graduate* and the mental health, co-dependency aspect of *Silver Linings*."

"Obviously," she agrees. "And there's a bit of something else too, I think. A little bit of unrequited love."

"Right, exactly," I agree. I have no idea what she is talking about, but my need to impress strangers with knowledge I do not necessarily possess is one of my weaknesses. *How am I supposed to learn from others if I cannot be honest about myself?* I must allow myself to feel less intelligent… less experienced… less worldly. "What's that exactly?"

Maya exhales, thinking of how to put the definition into plain speech. "It's basically one-sided love. Either the first person doesn't love the second person back, or the love is not *really* understood by first person to begin with. Maybe he or she is unaware of it."

"Okay," I nod. "That makes sense. So in *The Graduate*, Benjamin's love for Elaine is unrequited, at least at the beginning, and in *Silver Linings*, Bradley Cooper's character's love for his ex-wife is also unrequited."

"Exactly," she agrees. "And there are probably even more relationships in those two movies with similar traits that you could point to as well."

"That's interesting," I say. "I never really thought of unrequited love before, but it's kinda in a lot of movies."

Maya chuckles, "It's kinda in a lot of life."

I shrug. "I suppose."

"So Mr. Nerves doesn't have a problem with the ladies, is that what you're telling me?"

"I think every man alive has a problem with the ladies, in terms of fully understanding or appreciating them, but no – not in the way you speak of it."

"Good for you," she smiles. "At least that's one thing you don't have to be concerned about after high school." I grunt without thinking, which prompts her to pry. "Or maybe you do?"

"Kinda," I shift in my seat.

"Well, just lay it on me," she says. "I want to be able to help you with your paper, but I do have a life to get back to tonight."

I sigh. "I'm just nervous about how my relationship with Brianna – that's my girlfriend – how it will survive after high school. I'm going to stay here and live in Harlan while she goes off to college."

"Out of state?" she asks.

"Might as well be," I moan. "Nearly three hours away."

Maya forces a smile. "There's no easy answer to that. Either your relationship is meant to last or it isn't, and you're about to find out. Nothing will strengthen, or conversely destroy, a relationship like that amount of distance when you're eighteen years old."

"That's what I'm afraid of," I admit.

"Do you love her?" Maya asks.

"I do," I say with zero hesitation.

"To the best of your knowledge, does she love you? In the same way?"

"To the best of my knowledge, she does."

"Then I would say you have nothing to worry about," Maya says, leaning back into her seat.

"And yet that is all I am full of," I mumble.

"Are you the jealous type? Overly so?" she asks.

"Based on her looks, compared to mine, you would assume so, but no, I'm actually not," I state. "I'm just so grateful to be with her at all, I would honestly take any infidelities from her as a just repayment."

Maya furrows her brow. "You're not serious, are you?"

"I'm kidding, but only slightly," I answer.

"She must be some girl," Maya says, looking off toward the screen.

"She really is. She consumes my consciousness at all times." I pause and then ask, "Have you ever been in a relationship like that?" Maya stares ahead. I take her silence as offense given. "I'm sorry, I shouldn't have asked that."

"Me?" she says, still looking forward. "Oh, yeah. I was about your age."

I am not sure what it is – something about the look in her eyes, maybe – but I know I am not prepared for the story she is about to tell.

11

"When I was a freshman, I fell in love during my first-ever college class. His name was James, but everyone called him Mr. Weston. He was my literature professor.

"I walked into class that first day and found an empty seat in the middle of the second row. I didn't have any friends in that class, at least not yet, so I wanted to sit somewhat close to the front of the room so I had the opportunity to meet other students and maybe create some friendships. My rationale for sitting close to the front in class all changed when he walked in at eight o'clock, though.

"He appeared young for a professor, especially for something as dull as literature. He was tall, with wavy hair, and wore black-rimmed glasses. Even though it was only the first day, his eyes showed a high level of exhaustion behind those frames – the sort of exhaustion that comes from an unhappy life at home. I knew the look because I saw it on my father's face every day of my life growing up.

"When he walked in that day, he wouldn't even look at us until he had visited his desk. He spoke while conducting his morning tasks. 'Good morning, guys, and welcome to Lit 101' – and then he stopped. We locked eyes.

"We both knew the moment it happened, and neither one of us knew why it was happening. No one else around me seemed to be attracted to him in the way I was, or vice versa. It was just a moment of fate. We both felt it.

"He quickly looked away and began to conduct his first day the way he always had before – the way he planned it before he saw me. He handed out a syllabus, full of the books we would be reading and the due dates for various assignments we would be completing. I scanned the list of books, interested to see if I had read any before enrolling in the class, and there were a few notable ones, including the first book to be assigned to us – *1984*.

"He finished out class that day in a professional way, and he made sure to not make eye contact with me for the rest of the hour. Even after we were dismissed, he didn't watch me leave. I suspected that he would try to get one last good look at me as I walked away, as seemingly that's the sly move for every red-blooded male in the world. But he didn't. When I looked over my shoulder at him as I crossed the doorway, he was already sitting at his desk with his full attention on that day's newspaper.

"Any other girl would have just shrugged off what happened as a strange moment that meant nothing. Some sort of weird, vivid, yet fleeting, attraction. But I'm not any other girl. Regardless of our situations outside of school, I knew one thing after that first day –

"He had no chance."

"On Wednesday, I returned to class wearing skin-tight leggings and a crop-top tee shirt. No, it wasn't fair, exactly, but I just had to test the waters. I needed to know the truth about Mr. Weston. And the truth was apparent when we started reading *1984* in class.

"'If you're not familiar with the book, you are most certainly familiar with its themes – government control and overreach, the abuse of technology, the manipulation of a population via language, media, and warfare... it's all here,' he said, holding up the book. It's a great book, and, as he soon told us, it was Mr. Weston's favorite book as well.

"What I found most interesting in the book, though, wasn't the Big Brother stuff. It was the relationship between Winston, the book's protagonist, and Julia, his romantic interest. They engage in a sexual relationship for several reasons. There's the obvious reason, of course (*it's a jolly good time*), but there was another reason as well – a form of rebellion. I found that idea fascinating.

"Many students in the class were sort of confused by the characters' relationship, namely because Winston is not your typical 'catch.' He is off-beat, kind of a drag, and older than Julia. From what I can remember, Winston is about fifteen years older than her. My ears pricked up the moment I heard that number. Based on some social media 'research' I undertook the day before (of which there was barely any – he was all-but-off the grid), I knew Mr. Weston was thirty-four years old. Just as Winston was much older than Julia, Mr. Weston was years older than me.

"I took that as a sign. I know this all probably sounds childish, and even Ted Bundy-ish to some extent, but none of that was present in my motive. I wasn't driven by some dark force. I was not sexually, physically, or emotionally abused growing up. I did not have 'daddy' issues. I simply found my college professor to be handsome, charming, smart, and incredibly funny. He was everything I had been looking for."

"Things became complicated when I learned more about Mr. Weston's personal life. I wanted to get to know him better, to see if my feelings were valid or, more specifically, if they would be reciprocated. In order to do that, I had to spend as much time as possible with him outside of the classroom. So I set up several meetings with him – the kinds of meetings that are normal for any student to request. 'I'm struggling with this concept, do you think you could help me?' That sort of thing. And being a good, decent guy, he always obliged.

"Frankly, he showed no interest in me during those meetings. True, we had made a connection that first day of class. That was undeniable. But every day after that first one – *every moment* – Mr. Weston was adamant about maintaining his professionality. He helped me with my classwork when I requested it, and he treated me fairly. He never flirted or even looked me over while I pretended to look up answers in my textbook. But that all changed after I ran into him in the food court.

"I didn't plan it, but I happened to spot him as I walked through the line of restaurants at the student union one fall day. He was sitting alone and eating at Burger King, I believe. When I spotted him, I stopped and asked if I could join him. He looked around, as if he were worried about witnesses, but he obliged me. He was finishing his meal right as I was beginning mine, but he hung around anyway.

"He looked rough that day. Looked like he had slept all of four hours, at best, the night before, and his eyes were red. Being a college student, I knew the difference between red 'stoned' eyes and red 'teary' eyes, and he had the latter, though he would never admit that, of course. Instead of asking him anything directly, I made a bunch of small talk until he briskly cut me off.

"'Listen, I like talking to you, Maya. You're a smart girl with a bright future, but...'

"He struggled to finish any sentence that approached prying into someone else's feelings. 'But what?' I asked.

"'Why all of the interest?' he asked.

"'Interest?' I played dumb.

"'You're not a literature major, and yet you seem to be consumed with it and my class. I know there has to be something else going on. So I'll ask again... why all the interest?'

"'It's you,' I said plainly.

"'Me?' He was honestly baffled. 'Why me?'

"'Don't play games,' I insisted. 'You know we had a spark. On that first day of class. We locked eyes. Don't deny it.'

"'Listen,' he said as he stood abruptly. 'I apologize if I gave you that impression. My job is to teach and help you, just as I would any other student who is enrolled in my class.'

"'But I'm not any other student,' I said as he walked from the table. He stopped mid-stride and turned around.

"'I'm a married man, Maya,' he insisted firmly. 'I have kids. I have no intention of jeopardizing any of that.'

"'Why are your eyes so red?'

"'Excuse me?'

"'You heard me.'

"'This is absurd and, frankly, out of line.'

"'You're not a happy man, Mr. Weston.'

"And with that, he leaned in close to me and whispered, 'Who is?'

"After that, he turned and walked away. I finished my lunch alone and overwhelmed myself thinking about the mistake I had made. He was right. I was out of line. I had no right to try and corner him, let alone question his personal life. It was his job to help me, and I took advantage of his job description. No, he was right. I would apologize the next day."

"I went to class and slummed it up. I wore sweat pants, a hoodie, and my hair in a bun. I was as seductive as an old house slipper that had been shoved under the couch four years earlier and was now a mice haven. I didn't want to give any mixed signals. My goal was to apologize, plain and simple.

"During class, Mr. Weston never once looked at me. He conducted his class like he always did – concise, yet full of enough humor to engage us. It was as if the meeting at the food court never happened. When class ended, I watched from my desk as he packed up his things. Anyone could tell that he was in a hurry, but I was the only one who knew why.

"'About yesterday,' I began, 'I just wanted to apologize…'

"'It's quite all right,' he said, fully engaged in his task. He didn't even look up at me. When the door closed behind the final student, he looked around the empty room and then back at me. 'I understand that this can be a difficult time in your life. I get it. You're trying to figure out life and yet you still have that adventurous spirit in you. That's okay. But I can't be part of your adventure.'

"'I understand that now,' I nodded. 'I do apologize. It was wrong of me.'

"Mr. Weston nodded in agreement. 'Good, I'm glad.'

"An awkward silence surrounded us and, surprisingly, he was the first to break. 'Is everything okay? In your life, I mean.'

"'Sure,' I shrugged. 'I guess so. My, uh... whatever you want to call it... the food court thing... was not because of any issues or anything. I just...'

"'You just what?' he asked.

"'I just honestly felt a connection with you,' I sighed. 'I know it's wrong, but that's the honest truth. I never felt that instant connection with anyone before in my life. Ever.' He remained silent and still, but I could tell that his brain was nodding in agreement. 'Haven't you ever felt that way?'

"'Sure,' he said, taking a seat behind his desk. We were becoming more relaxed. I pulled up a chair in front of his desk. 'I felt that with my wife, when we first met.'

"'I always thought that's how it should be,' I said. 'That's how you know you found true love. You don't need to say anything. It's just a lightning bolt that you have to ride and not get struck by instead.'

"'That's an interesting way to look at it,' he agreed. 'Sort of violent, though.'

"'Well, what causes more violence than love?' I asked.

"'Touché,' he acknowledged. Another silence.

"'Did you ride the lightning?' I asked.

"'Yeah,' he laughed. 'For a while anyway.' With that comment, he knew he had screwed up. He began to stand again, but I promptly stopped him.

"'Wait,' I insisted. 'What does that mean?'

"'It doesn't mean anything.'

"'I'm just trying to adjust to adulthood… the world.'

"'I can help you adjust to literature, and that's about it.'

"'Why do you always look so tired?'

"That question gave him pause. He shook his head. 'Tired?' he asked in an ironic, exhausted breath.

"'Yeah,' I continued. 'Your eyes are always red like you haven't slept in days and you ingest coffee as though you're being paid to taste test it.'

"'I sleep just fine, and who drinks more coffee than teachers? Even I'll admit that it's kinda cliché at this point.'

"'If you sleep just fine, then why are your eyes always red? Especially in the morning?'

"With that, he leaned in and stared into my eyes in a way he never had before. 'What do you want me to say? That my life is difficult? That I am *eternally* sad? Unfulfilled? Stuck in a loveless marriage? Fine, there you go. You win.' He began opening and shutting desk drawers for no apparent reason other than to seem busy in the moment and to divert his attention away from me. 'It's the first freakin' month of class…' he mumbled to himself amid drawer slams.

"'I'm not trying to *win* anything…'

"'It seems as though you are,' he nearly shouted as he looked back up at me. 'You're prying into my life as if you think you can help me or something, but the truth is you're a college student and I am a professor in my thirties. My problems are real. I am constantly worried about increases in my healthcare premiums because I have to provide for my wife and two kids. You're worried about not becoming Instagram famous or pulling in the acceptable amount of followers, comments, or likes. There's no comparison between our lives' problems.'

"If you really think that's who I am, then you're mistaken. I could give a shit about social media. I'm worried about my entire life. Finishing this degree, finding a job, starting a life, buying a house, connecting with someone… While you have most of your life figured out, I have almost none of mine.'

"We stared at each other. Finally, he said, 'I apologize. You're right. That was a mean generalization on my part. I remember being your age. I was just trying to emphasize the difference in our lives. Why talking to each other outside of class is a mistake.'

"'Well, to me, digging yourself an early grave because of stress is the bigger mistake. If you're unhappy, do something about it.'

"'That's not how life works. Not in the adult world.'

"'What about one moment?' I asked.

"'One moment?' he said. 'Of what?'

"'I'm not trying to turn your life upside down, I just want to know about one moment,' I requested. 'Would that change anything?'

"'One moment as in…' he looked around as if he were Nixon being wiretapped in his own office. '…*one moment* one moment?'

"'Yeah,' I stated simply. 'Isn't that what it's all about? Isn't it better to have one moment with someone, even if it's fleeting, than to disregard it and have none at all?'

"'That's about all it would take at this point,' he mumbled. 'Sorry, I shouldn't have said that. My filter weakens more each day.'

"'That's what I'm talking about, though,' I said, leaning forward on my desk. 'You're such a good dude…'

"'Oh, wow, thank you,' he said sarcastically. 'I hope they use that in my eulogy.'

"'For real, though,' I insisted. 'You deserve better. You deserve someone who appreciates you. Who *wants* you.'

"The heaviness of the moment sank in. 'Is that it?' he finally asked slowly. 'You *want* me?'

"I had never been so bold in my life, especially with a man. But there was something unique about Mr. Weston. He brought out the id in me, as Freud would say. I was all about making bad and impulsive decisions in that moment.

"I stood up from my desk and walked over behind his. I leaned down and looked him directly in the eyes. 'That's exactly what I want.'

"The next time I saw Mr. Weston was in class the following Monday, and that day was one of the most tension-filled of my life. I had no intention of holding back. I knew I could finally get through to him that day. As he lectured, he kept gazing over at me as though he were preparing for battle. Just like a soldier, he knew he would either find new life through me, or death.

"When class ended, I slowly gathered my things and walked up to his desk. Three other students hung around after class that day to request help – two girls and one guy. I hung back behind them, continually making eyes with Mr. Weston as he tried his best to help the other wayward students. It was a done deal, and he knew it.

"I never tout my own beauty, but I looked *good* that day. I wore heavy mascara and eye shadow to bring out my eyes, which had often been named among my 'top three best features' on anonymous Snapchat comments, even before that day. I wore my hair down and straight, and despite the chilly weather, I wore a short sun dress. It took every muscle in Mr. Weston's body to resist gawking at my legs (number two of my 'top three best features') during those minutes right after class. His face was literally turning red from straining. One of the yokels requesting help even asked if he was okay.

"'I'm okay,' he reassured him, 'I just, uh, I have to help out Maya here, too, before I head out today.'

"The other students turned around and saw the smoke show that was me. Perhaps picking up on what I was putting down, they decided it was time to go to their next class. Once the three stooges were out of the room, I walked over to Mr. Weston's desk. He was still seated behind it. For the time being.'

"'Maya, it's good to...' he trailed off as he finally let his eyes gaze upon me. The relief was instant in his face, as was his growing reaction.

"'Your eyes are red again,' I said softly, as I moved in closer.

"'Yeah, I had kinda a rough night,' he stammered as he tried to compose himself. You could practically hear his inner monologue repeating out loud, *Don't do this, Don't do this, DON'T DO THIS.*

"'Do you enjoy being sad?' I asked. 'Is that it?'

"'*Enjoyment* might be the wrong word, but it does help fuel my life in a weird way,' he babbled almost incoherently. He seemed to enjoy talking to me for once, as it diverted attention away from his growing problem.

"'You can go back to being sad soon,' I said as I stood directly above him, 'but right now, you're going to feel good.'

"'Don't do this,' his inner monologue finally spilled out as he tried to push me away. 'You don't understand how weak I really am...' he murmured in a way that almost made me feel sorry for him. *Almost.*

"'What, *this*?' I asked as I lowered myself down and straddled his leg. 'You can't resist me, no matter your reasons or higher understanding.'

"Our eyes locked as solidly together as our bodies did. We both felt the tension of the moment... the wrongness... the sheer *excitement*. We stared at each other for what felt like an eternity but was probably only ten seconds in real time. It all came down to my original question.

"*Did we want a moment together or miss out on it forever?*

"'This is all up to you, Chief,' I said, looking down at him as I moved along his leg. 'You have to make the move or else this is all it'll ever be.'

"Given the ultimatum, he lunged forward and swept me up into a kiss. The moment was so frenzied and lustful and chaotic that I thought his chair was spinning out of control. In actuality, the only direction it was going was backwards. We fell onto the ground and erupted in laughter. As we lay there, though, the laughter died as a new desire was born. He looked up at me and ran his fingers through my hair. I had never felt such admiration in my life. I know I sound like some sort of home-wrecking sex deviant, but the truth was he felt that same exact desire for me. He was just too ashamed to admit that he could ever be weak enough to let something like that happen. But it did.

"I happened."

"Just like that, James and I began a relationship. Sure, it was kept a secret, but it was a relationship nonetheless. It was more than that, though. It was fiery… passionate… lustful… all of the romantic adjectives. It was everything, and we enjoyed every minute of it.

"We kept up appearances in class. No one ever knew there was anything going on between us. Sure, I would tease him sometimes from my seat, but he always kept himself composed. The most he ever gave me was a slight smirk, and that was only when I really pushed the boundaries of classroom etiquette.

"Once class was over, though, it was a frenzy. We would lunge at each other like rival alpha primates competing for dominance of land. Our lust was almost violent in a way. It took all of our willpower to hold back our passion, but once we had an opportunity, we always took it.

"We would meet in his classroom, in his office, or sometimes even in his car during 'after hours.' Yeah, I know that doesn't exactly make me Miss Romance, but it was always my choice. And this is real life, not a movie. If you're going to hook up with a married man, it's going to be in an inconvenient spot.

"But therein lay the problem. As much as I wanted to pretend that our love was special or was going to transcend the norms of everyday society, I always had to deal with that fact. James was a married man with a family. It made my stomach turn every time I thought about it. I usually tried to do everything I could to avoid thinking about it, because when I did, my stomach roiled. *What was I doing? Was I really this person? Had my parents taught me nothing?*

"Six months into our relationship, we both felt the inevitable. It had been a fun ride, but that's all it had been – an amusement park adventure. A log ride, if you will. What we had was not sustainable. It was childish escapism that eventually had to come to an end.

"I knew it was all over the night he texted me to come to his office. It was on a Tuesday, and our meetups never occurred on Tuesdays or Thursdays. As I walked to campus that night, I decided that I would be the one to end it. I had gotten him into this mess, and I would be the one to get him out. It was all my fault, after all.

"When I arrived at his door, I slowly pushed it open and found him behind his desk. His eyes were red again, revealing the sadness that had been absent on his face since our first escapade in his classroom. He asked me to sit down.

"'Before you begin,' I said, 'I just want to say something.'

"'Sure, go ahead,' he agreed.

"I took a breath. 'It's over, James. We both know it. But it's okay.'

"'It's okay?' he nearly scoffed. 'What do you mean?'

"'I asked you for a moment – a moment to connect with you because I had never felt that way before. You brought something out in me. Something more than what I imagine you're even thinking. You made me feel comfortable about becoming an adult. I had been terrified of that idea for as long as I can remember, but because of you, I'm no longer scared. I know that I can make it through life, because anything should be easy now.'

"'Why is that?' he asked.

"'Because if I can live without you, then I can make it through anything,' I said.

"James's eyes filled with tears. He looked away from me. 'I told her,' he said to the wall.

"'*You told your wife about us?*' I asked in astonishment.

"'Yes and no,' he replied. He took a breath that felt painful even from my perspective. 'I told her that I had been unfaithful.'

"'And?' was all I could muster.

"'Well, she was pissed to say the least.'

"'I can imagine. It's been six months, James…'

"'No,' he said simply.

"'No?'

"'No. It was one time. I got drunk at the faculty Christmas party that she couldn't attend because she was out of town at her sister's. I was upset that night and drank more than usual... more than I should have. And that night, I made a mistake. One mistake.'

"'So you condensed our long love affair down into a single night? You created a new lie?' He simply nodded his head. I was stunned by his explanation. I was somehow offended by it, even though I had no right to be. 'A mistake?' was all I could say next.

"Finally, he stopped talking to the wall and looked back at me. We locked eyes again, just as we had that first day in class. I was too afraid to admit it in the moment, but I loved him. I loved him since that first day in class. I knew, though, that I should never admit that to him. And that night was, perhaps, the worst possible time to bring up the idea of love.

"'You were not a mistake,' he clarified. 'My mistake was in thinking I could maintain this double life... that I could put myself before my...' He didn't finish, but I knew he was talking about his kids. And that's what made me feel the shittiest. I had jeopardized his relationship with his kids. I never wanted that. He was a good father. I just happened to love him as well.

"'I'm the one who made the mistake,' I replied. 'This is all on me.'

"'Absolutely not,' he stated firmly. 'That is bullshit. I was the weak one. I knew better.'

"'That may be true, but nothing could have stopped me from pursuing you,' I explained. 'I regret that this got carried away, but I don't regret making a connection with you.' I paused to compose myself, because I knew the next thing I had to say would be difficult. 'You meant everything to me, and I will never be the same again.'

"I stood up from his desk. I was once again initiating the end. 'Is your marriage going to survive?'

"He contemplated the thought. 'Yeah, I think so. Having kids makes it difficult to actually end a marriage, but I think we're going to try and make it work.'

"I didn't want to pry any more than I already had – to plant doubt more than I already had – but I am bad at impulse control, as you might have guessed. 'Do you want it to work?'

"'I love my kids,' he said with zero hesitation. 'More than anything.'

"We shared a gaze and I decided it was finally time to go. Forever. I turned and placed my hand on the doorknob as he stood from his desk.

"'Maya?' he said softly.

"I kept my hand on the door but turned my body toward him. 'Yeah?'

"'I wish this could have been different…' he began to ramble aimlessly.

"'I know,' I said. 'Me too.'

"'I just want you to know something,' he said, closing the distance between us. I dropped my hand and turned toward him fully. He looked down at me from his tall stature, the thing I always found so sexy about him… his ability to physically and emotionally shield me from the world.

"'What's that?' I asked, trying to play off my desire to jump into his embrace.

"'In another lifetime, we would have worked. I don't want you to think less of yourself because of the poor decisions we made. We acted out on them because of a primal desire. That does not excuse them, but they were hard to suppress. We shared an intimacy that I never fathomed possible. If I were younger or you were older…'

"'Down with Big Brother,' I said.

"'What do you mean?' he asked. He had not yet put it all together, but I imagine he did later that night.

"'It's okay,' I said, looking up at him. 'Really. You don't have to say anything else. I'm a big girl. I knew what I was getting involved with.'

"'You just deserve better than this,' he said. 'This mess. Me. This whole thing. I hope you understand that. And even though we are going to live our separate lives now, I know I will always think of you when I have trouble sleeping at night… in those hours when the realms of dreams and reality intertwine and challenge each other. I will always wonder where you are.'

"'I know this is inappropriate, but what's one more?' I said as I grabbed him into an embrace and kissed him for the last time. Being the man he is, he didn't engage fully with me, but he didn't deny me either, and that said everything about our relationship. 'I'll miss you, James. Thank you for giving me my moment.'"

12

I am motionless after Maya finishes recounting her sordid love affair with her college professor. First off, as an introvert, I would never open up in the way she did just now – *least of all* to a stranger. I cannot help but wonder why she did, and yet I am too afraid to ask her directly.

"I'm sure you're wondering why I told you all of that," she says.

Welp, that takes care of that.

"Uh, yeah, kinda," I stammer. "I mean, I'm not judging you, I just…"

"It's because you have that lost look in your eye," she explains. "I recognized it as soon as you sat down next to me. I had those same eyes for years. It sucks."

"So… how are your eyes now?" I ask like a goof.

She laughs. "Well, they're not as lost, I guess. And it's because of the story I just told you. A person really gets to know herself when she goes through something like that."

"Yeah, I can only imagine," I agree. "What did you…?"

"Discover about myself?"

"Yeah."

"That I am better off like this," she gestures toward the theater screen.

"What do you mean?" I ask. "Alone?"

"Yeah, basically," she shrugs. "I should probably apologize. I know I laid a lot on you tonight, and you're just asking questions for some… What was it again?"

I stare blankly. "Oh, me? Oh, it's, uh, for my, uh, college entry, um, essay…"

"Right," she says a tad unconvinced. "It's just these movies, especially the first one. It really reminds me of James. Or Professor Weston, as I should probably call him now."

"Is it more than just the age difference thing?" I ask. "I mean, obviously, the big thing about *The Graduate* is that it's about a love affair between a young adult and a middle-aged woman, so I can see that. But is there something more?"

"Yeah, it's like I was saying earlier," she explains. "The whole unrequited love thing. My love for James was essentially one-sided."

"I'm not sure you can say that," I think aloud. "Based on what you said, he seemed more than willing to engage with you."

"Sure, after a while," she scoffs. "After I threw myself at him. Literally. But some guys like that, you know? He was a person of authority who had his authority challenged. Some guys like when a woman is assertive, takes charge, doesn't ask questions, is a tad aggressive… you know what I mean?"

I start to sweat. "Oh, sure, I mean, yeah, I assume there are guys like that… there are guys everywhere who all like different things, and, um… you know, I would never judge someone for liking what they like, after all… I mean, I have my own things going on…"

"Settle down, Beavis," Maya laughs. "I'm not asking you what your kink is. I was just explaining myself. What it came down to, though, was… it just wasn't right between us."

"Well, it's kinda hard…" I begin to say with a bit of a scoff. *Let's not forget about his side of things, after all.*

"Because he had a family?" she cuts me off. She exhales loudly and sinks low into her seat. "I should never have done what I did. I just… I felt that sensation, you know? That longing for someone you deeply connect with. Someone who is similar and yet different enough to challenge you and make life exciting. It's hard to let that feeling go. In a moment like that, you feel as though anything is possible."

"Do you regret hooking up with him?" I ask.

"I do," she says without hesitation. "I could have wrecked his entire life. Sure, his wife may have been a monster who made him feel worthless, but it wasn't my job to come in and save him. I do regret pushing him into our relationship, but I don't regret feeling love toward him or for telling him about those feelings, because they were *real*. My feelings toward him were just as tangible as that movie screen is to us right now. I could see them plainly, and I certainly felt them. I still do."

"Have you talked to him since?"

"Not once. I've come close many times. I mostly feel that desire to speak to him when life gets complicated. I want to feel his guidance and warmth again. I've written enough text messages and emails to fill a book, but I always delete them right after they are fully composed."

"Why not send him a message? I know it's not proper…"

"That's exactly why. That's not how our society works. We are allowed to feel whatever we want throughout the day, but we are only allowed to act on a small portion of those feelings. The acceptable ones must be morally and societally acceptable first and foremost, and reaching out to a married father is just not one of those accepted things."

"I can understand that," I say. "Would it help if you used me?"

"I'm sorry?" Maya asks.

"Well, you'll never email or text him again, right?"

"Right."

"So why don't you just tell me what you would tell him? It might make you feel better to get it all out, and there would be no repercussions. It's not like I'm gonna go call him up."

"What if you go and put all of my dirty laundry in your little college essay?"

"I can assure you that I would never do that."

Maya looks me over. "Okay, Guy. Let me ask you one thing first."

"Sure thing," I say willingly.

"Dirty confessions aren't your kink, right?" she says, squinting at me. "You're not gonna go use me…"

"I don't have a kink!" I shout. No one else is currently in the theater, but I can't help but wonder if Caitlyn and Kylie heard that. I know for a fact they are doing their best to eavesdrop.

"If you say so," Maya says with a wink.

13

"I've been wanting to talk to you for a while now, James. I've just found it difficult to…" Maya stops abruptly. "Is it okay if I call you James? Is that weird? I just want to stay in character, or whatever."

"No, it's fine," I appease. "Call me whatever. Pretend I am James in this moment."

"I bet you wish I would," she chuckles. "You're a little deviant, aren't you?"

"No!" I nearly shout again. "You just make me feel as though I am. Please, continue."

I would never say this to Maya directly, but it is no wonder James, or Mr. Weston, could not deny her after being tested for so long. She has such a persistent, seductive drive. She creates a pain in me that is hard to overcome. I do not think any man could battle her desires. She could best anyone.

"I have written you so many times because you were always so easy to talk to… to share my problems with. I miss your kindness and guidance. I miss your dry sense of humor and your quick wit. I miss seeing you every other day, whether it was in your classroom, in your office, or in your car…"

I begin to sweat again.

"…Wherever I saw you became the new center of my universe. I loved walking into any room that you were in – the way you lit up when you saw me again. No one ever responded to me the way you did. You were my favorite thing in this world. I wish I could find someone else – I really do. I long to feel the way I felt about you about anyone. That *need* to simply see your face to make me feel better. You could turn any bad day around for me. I even miss seeing you sad."

What? Maybe I should actually be concerned here. She does sound a bit Ted Bundy-ish...

"I knew you were sad because you were miserable in all of the moments that you weren't around me or your kids. At least that's what you told me. I miss trying to make you feel better. I never felt useful before I met you, and I haven't ever since. You gave me purpose. I knew our relationship was always going to be short-lived, but I wish more than anything that it could have been longer. Just a *little* longer. But that's the thing – it would never have been enough."

She takes a breath as I discreetly slide my phone out of my pocket and dial 9-1-1 just in case she goes full *Fatal Attraction*.

"Because of that, it's probably good that it ended when it did. I'm not sorry that I told you about my feelings, but I am sorry I pursued you the way I did."

That's better. She's sounding more reasonable, I suppose. I put my phone away.

"That wasn't fair of me. I'll always love you, James, but from afar."

She finishes her verbal letter with a *whew*.

"Feel better?" I ask.

She slowly turns her head toward me. "Actually, I kinda do. Thanks, Guy."

"No problem," I say, smiling.

Maya's energy increases once that burden is lifted. "So how can I help you out? I made you sit through all of my personal gar-baj, it's the least I can do."

"Honestly," I say, "I think you helped me more than you realize."

"How so?" she asks.

"I don't want my girlfriend to go to college and leave me behind, but if our relationship can't sustain that, then it was never meant to be. Some things are just burdens you can't overcome. Distance may be mine, just like…"

"An extramarital affair was mine?"

I fall silent. "Well, yeah, in so many words."

Maya laughs. "Ease up. You're not gonna hurt my feelings."

"Sorry."

"Stop apologizing, Guy."

"Sorry. Err, I mean…"

"You're exhausting," she chuckles. "I think distance might be a secondary concern for you. Did I really make you feel better, though?"

"Sure," I answer. "It's just like in *Silver Linings Playbook*. Pat is obsessed with winning his ex-wife back. He is so consumed by her that he even neglects the beautiful woman in front of him because he is so blinded by his own unrequited love for that past love. But once he took those blinders off, he realizes that there might be even greater things out there that await him."

"According to your theory then, someone better than your girlfriend might be out there."

I am offended that Maya comes to that conclusion, but her reasoning, based on my analysis of the movie, is correct. "Well, I highly doubt that…"

"*And*," she continues, "Someone better than James awaits me?"

"Well, it may not be another man…"

"Interesting…"

Sweat begins to trickle again.

"No, I didn't mean it like that," I quickly correct. "The greater thing may not be another relationship. It may be something else you need instead. Something else you need even more."

"All of a sudden, you're acting wise for your age," she smirks. "What do you think I need even more than a new and improved relationship."

"Honestly, I think you need someone to talk to," I say frankly.

"Okay, well I rambled on at great length earlier, so go ahead and explain yourself."

"It's like in *The Graduate*. Benjamin constantly faces questions and judgements from his family and neighbors. They all want to hear about what is next for him, what he plans on doing now that he's graduated, and when he plans to officially begin his life. Of course, the problem is that Ben doesn't know any of those answers. The more the 'grown-ups' harass him, the more he withdraws and begins making poor life decisions, like the other 'adults' that surround him. Everyone expects Ben to know those answers already, and they get upset with him when he shows uncertainty. Now, I don't really know you, Maya… well, I know *a lot* about you now, much of which I won't soon forget, but if I had to guess, I would say that not a lot of people checked in on you once you made that leap into 'adulthood.' So, you started to make those poor life decisions. The ones we see adults make around us every single day."

Maya evaluates me. I can tell she does not quite appreciate having the therapist's chair turned on her, but she goes with it for the time being. "Go ahead, Freud."

"All I'm saying is that if those same adults in *The Graduate* had checked in on Ben earlier and helped him navigate that transition to adulthood, then he would have had a better chance at becoming a well-adjusted adult. But because they didn't, he not only struggles but takes the blame."

"Continue, if you have more to say," she states.

"Adults are just like that. They pretend that they have it all figured out. Nothing stresses them out, nothing depresses them, nothing can kill their drive. But it's all a lie. No one has anything figured out, at least from what I can tell. If adults were honest with themselves, they'd admit that they didn't have life figured out, and because they have so much more experience than we do, they'd admit that it's okay if we don't either. No one wants to hang around 'professional' adults anyway. We like honest adults who question life, who are honest, who are independent and full of life."

"Where do you think I can find one of these honest, fun-loving adults to rent?" she says. "I could use one."

"I'll let you know when I find one," I answer. "But that's my point. We're all searching for someone to hang onto… to feel safe and secure. I don't want to presume anything, but I can only assume that's why you were so drawn to Mr. Weston. He was older, had experience, and could make you feel better about the things that concerned you. It doesn't have to be about love, though. It just has to be a connection with someone else."

"Sounds like you have it all figured out then," she shrugs. "Doesn't your girlfriend, Britanna…?"

"Brianna."

"…Brianna help fill that void in you?"

"Of course she does. That's why I'm afraid of losing her." I fall silent after blurting that out. I do not know if I had ever spoken those words out loud before, but they have been rattling around in my head for months now. It kind of feels good to vocalize them for once.

"If she is the one – the one to make you feel that way, as you described – then I have no doubt it'll work out, Guy," Maya reassures me.

"You really think so?" I ask for extra reassurance.

"I do."

We share a moment of comfortable silence. *What is left to say after all of that?* And just as that thought occurs to me, Maya seems to feel it, too, and stands.

"Well, this has been… *something*, Guy," Maya says, putting on her winter coat. "I hope I gave you something useful for your essay."

I stand as well. "You certainly did."

We begin to walk sideways out of the row of seats, and I follow her out of the theater toward the exit. I look up at the clock as we enter the lobby and notice that Maya and I have talked for more than an hour. All of the other employees must have given up on us and went home. Their punishment for keeping them as long as I did was to leave to me to lock up the building on my own. I, however, willingly accept that punishment.

I open the door for Maya. "Hey, can I ask you one more question before you leave?"

"Not sure I have anything left to say that I haven't already told you, but you can try," she replies.

"Why do you come to the movies alone?" I ask.

She turns from the cold and faces me. "Because it's the only time I can fully let go. Of everything. I can enjoy something without feeling like I need to think about what stresses me out, or to think about my failures. To think about what could have been." She trails off. "Surely you see a lot of people like me here."

"I do," I say. "And I'm one of them, too."

"I thought you might be," she says. She then turns back toward the still-open exit door.

"Thanks for talking to me tonight," I say, extending my arm to hold open the door.

"Thanks for listening to me blabber and, more importantly, not judging me."

I guiltily think of almost emergency-dialing as she recited her letter but quickly disregard the thought. "You're not a bad person. You just need someone."

"Someone to talk to," she says tugging a stocking cap over her head.

"I'm always willing, if you don't mind indulging a high school senior," I add.

She smiles. It is the same brutally beautiful smile that inevitably slayed Professor Weston. "I don't mind. Want to give me your number?"

For whatever reason – either feeling guilty about giving another girl my phone number or feeling cocky for the first time in my life – I decide to play it cool. "You know where to find me."

As I close the door to the theater, Maya abruptly stops it one last time. "Hey, Guy?"

"Yeah?"

"Remember – you're not a high school senior anymore. You're a graduate."

14

I did not get the theater fully closed down until around one o'clock this morning, but my experiment last night was, in my estimation at least, a success. The only downside to my still-in-practice theory is that I have to be back at work sooner than I would have liked today.

I unlock the theater doors at noon. Since it is a Sunday, we will show an early matinee that, usually, appeases our more elderly patrons, but today is a bit different.

I am in a good mood, not just because of last night's success, but because both Caitlyn and Kylie are working alongside me today. Margie and Ronnie take Sundays off to go to church, eat fried chicken, and then nap before *60 Minutes* comes on.

Caitlyn arrives at the theater at one o'clock on the dot, her assigned time, and Kylie arrives at one twenty – twenty minutes past hers. Caitlyn and I agree to hold off on all conversations about my escapade until Kylie arrives just so we do not have to go over everything twice.

"How'd it go last night?" Kylie asks the moment she bursts through the door.

Caitlyn and I are awaiting this moment comfortably on the bottom of the left staircase. "Surprisingly well," I respond.

"Well, you're gonna have to give more than that," Kylie continues. "Mainly, what I'm asking is… *did I nail it*? Am I a good judge of character or what?"

I recall Maya's many-faceted character. There is a lot to go over, and I have been doing just that ever since our conversation ended last night. "A 'good judge of character' might be misleading," I say, "but Maya definitely enlightened me last night."

Kylie plops down on the steps behind Caitlyn and me. "Oooh, so this 'Maya' was a bit of a freak, eh?"

"How did you get that from what I said?" I scoff.

"Well, you *did say* she 'enlightened you last night,' Guy," Caitlyn adds. "That sounds overly vague and somehow like a Victorian romance."

Fair point.

"I didn't mean to say that I fell in love with her or anything," I clarify. "I just meant that she helped me out a lot. Maya told me things I definitely needed to hear."

"Like, 'Come here, big boy,'" Kylie teases. "I bet she gave you an education, all right. A bachelor's in plowing fine ass…"

"Kylie, come on!" I laugh. "I would never do that. You know better."

"Yeah, I know," she admits. "You're lame like that."

"I'm lame because I love Brianna," I mutter.

"No, you're lame because you wouldn't make a move on her for the story," she says. "At least lie to us for a bit, and make us think something *scandalous* happened. That would have been more fun, and it would have killed half our day. Imagine the fun we could have had… the scenarios you could have painted for us..."

"Sorry, I didn't think about your needs, Kylie," I apologize sarcastically.

"Yeah, well, no one does," she mumbles. She looks over at the concession stand. "Did you have any leftover corn from last night?"

I knew this was coming. "Yes," I say, exhausted. "It's in a bag for you already, on the counter next to the register."

Kylie jumps over the concession counter easily, and grabs the bag of popcorn. *Maybe her track coach was wrong... Maybe she just needed motivation?*

"That's so disgusting," Caitlyn says. "I still can't get over your obsession with stale popcorn."

"There's nothin' better than day-old corn, I'm tellin' you guys," Kylie says through a mouthful.

"We still showing that animated movie for the matinee?" Caitlyn asks me.

"Yep," I nod.

"Ain't no old-timer gonna show up for that," Kylie says and then suppresses a violent burp.

"Nope," I shake my head.

"So, what are we gonna do with no customers today?" Caitlyn asks.

"We could order a pie and make some TikToks," Kylie excitedly shouts, spitting out niblets of corn.

"Ew, slow down, Kyle!" Caitlyn exclaims. "We know you're the TikTok queen."

"Damn right."

"Fine, let's do it," I say as I hop to my feet. Both Kylie and Caitlyn look shocked at my enthusiastic response. No, making TikToks is not my ideal version of fun, but it is a distraction. And I need all the distractions I can get at the moment, especially if they involve my friends.

I did not text Brianna this morning. Even though I proclaimed my love for her to both my coworkers and to Maya last night, I did not feel like talking to her today. I am not sure why. Sometimes I get this way. Sometimes I want her to get mad at me. To think I am not okay. To think that something is wrong. Wrong with us.

Why is that?
Because you're a moron.
Well, yeah, but why else?
Because you want to make it easier.
For whom?
Both of you.

"Hey 'Awakenings,' are you coming?" Kylie shouts. "We need you to do this dance with us. Our videos get more likes when you're in them. I think people feel sorry for you and your abilities." She pauses to elocute. "How do I say this? My followers think you're like one of those people who asks a celebrity to his high school prom, and the celebrity needs to avoid bad press because of a recent scandal, so she makes a sweet video in response that kindly turns him down, but in a flirty, fun way. You know what I mean?"

"Be right there," I grumble.

Rip the Band-Aid off.

PART THREE

PAPER MOON

BIRDMAN

15

"Why are you being such a jerk?" Brianna screams at me through the phone.

"Because I have to work and you're making me feel guilty about it," I answer back with attitude.

"No, that is not why," she answers back adamantly. "I'm upset with you because you won't talk to me about what's bothering you."

"Nothing's bothering me."

"And yet you can talk to Cate and Kyle about everything, but not your girlfriend."

"So now you're jealous of them?"

"Um, no. Absolutely not. I love them. And I love you. You're just being stubborn right now, and I'm trying to figure out why."

"Maybe I don't want to be bothered. Maybe I just want to feel the way I do and be okay with that. Maybe I don't want to hear a hundred questions about how I'm feeling every day. That's what you do, B – you badger. Badger, badger, badger."

"Okay, I'll stop asking how you're doing then. You've obviously got it figured out."

"Right."

"And what about me?"

"What about you?"

"What about how I feel? What if I need someone to talk to? What if I need to vent my feelings?"

"I'll listen to you, but I just can't deal with it right now – right this second – as I'm walking into work."

"Okay, so when it's convenient for you, I can talk to you."

"Correct."

"You're being such a jerk."

"That's just you're opinion. I think I'm being honest."

"Maybe I'll just find someone else to talk to then."

———

What the hell is wrong with you?
Shut up.
No, I won't.
Well, you should.
You're a scumbag.
I've been called worse.
Yeah, by me – which is you. Scumbag.
I hate you.
That's pretty obvious at this point. You've got some issues, pal.
Silence.
Why did you talk to her that way?
She was being annoying. I hate it when she gets like that.
She was not being "annoying." She was checking in on you and you totally blew her off.
So?
She'll leave you.
She will anyway.
THAT'S what this is…

Oh, so now you're smart?

What a hero. You're such a man, taking care of this problem nice and early...

You know what? I am a hero. I'm taking care of it so that she doesn't have to. Because of me, she won't have to feel guilty later on about dumping me. Starting a new, better life.

Silence.

You've got nothing to say to that?

No – you don't.

I'm confused.

Same.

Why do we do this?

Because you lack relationship, and overall people, skills. And because you're an idiot.

Oh, yeah.

And because you're a bad boyfriend. Bordering on bad person in general.

I know...

So act differently.

I know...

Why don't you? You know she loves you.

I know!

Silence.

What?

That was shouty.

Sorry.

She does love you.

I know. That's why it's so scary.

You're making a mistake.

I...

"Are you high?" Kylie asks.

"Huh?" I ask, sounding high.

"What are you doing?" Caitlyn asks.

I look around and notice that I'm standing at the top of the theater's staircase. "Oh, nothing, I was just going to check the projector."

"Why, though?" Kylie asks.

"If I'm going to inherit this old building and everything within, I want to make sure the equipment is working as efficiently as possible," I say, attempting to sound authoritative as I continue my way upstairs.

"You might want to check on yourself then!" Kylie shouts from below.

I wander into the projection booth. I have a long night ahead of me. It is double-feature night. I cannot afford to lose a grip on my psyche this early *and* in public. I suppress all of my inner turmoil for the time being and focus instead on the projector.

Just then, Caitlyn walks into the booth as well. I pretend to tinker with something that I know nothing about. My lack of education is apparent.

"What's going on with you?" she asks in a near-whisper.

"Nothing, I'm just…" I say, busy at fake-work.

"Don't give me that," Caitlyn pushes my shoulder. "Brianna just texted me. What's up?"

I sigh. "I honestly don't know. I… just don't know."

Caitlyn tries to empathize, but with the way I am acting, I imagine she is finding it difficult. "It's double-feature night, right? What's the line-up?"

Clearly she is trying to talk movies with me to make me feel better. I appreciate the gesture, but I can't help but think it might be pointless. "We're starting with *Hud*, followed by *Whiplash*."

"What's *Hud*?" she asks. "I don't know that one."

"It stars Paul Newman as an alcoholic, mean, arrogant rancher – 'Hud' – who constantly pushes his father, played by Melvin Douglas, to his limits. Hud abuses any kindness others show him just so he can make more money, date more married women, drink more booze, get in more fights… you get the idea."

"Interesting," Caitlyn feigns. "How does that align with *Whiplash*? That's the one with the jazz drummer, right?"

"Right, from 2014," I confirm. "They mesh because they both have characters that will not stop until they get what they want. Miles Teller's character won't stop until he is the legendary drummer he desires to be, and J.K. Simmons, as the instructor, won't stop pushing his student until he is the drummer he knows he can be."

"I see," Caitlyn says. "Kind of a darker theme today."

"Maybe a little bit," I agree.

Caitlyn sways on her feet, her innocent way of trying to soften a statement that could be construed as offensive to the receiver.

"What?" I ask. "Just ask me."

"Maybe you should switch the line-up tonight," she suggests.

"Switch the movies?" I ask incredulously. "This close before showtime? That's not a good idea. What about the pre-sale tickets…?"

"That we've sold none of so far?" she finishes. "I think it'll be okay. Our double feature audience comes no matter what we play."

"Why are you suggesting this?" I ask.

"I think you could use some more inspiring themes tonight," she says. "Plus, weren't you wanting to show *La La Land* soon? You can't show two Damien Chazelle movies back-to-back."

I stare, understanding for the first time that she may be playing me for a fool more than I realize. "How do you know who directed *Whiplash* and *La La Land*."

She shrugs. "I work at a movie theater."

"You're too smart for your own good. You really are."

"What do you think?" she asks, stepping toward our makeshift BluRay and 4K UHD shelf we have in our projection booth. "Can you think of a way to pair two different movies to screen tonight on such short notice?"

She is clearly challenging me… testing my movie knowledge. I cannot refuse the challenge. "I probably could."

Caitlyn is silent for a few seconds, until she knows she finally has the clearance to say what she has been really wanting to ask. "You know what you're doing isn't right, don't you?"

"What am I doing?" I ask.

"You're pushing Brianna away," she says.

"How would you know anything about what's going on between us?"

"I get a sense of things."

"She talked to you, didn't she?"

Caitlyn shrugs. "We *are* friends."

I shake my head in frustration. "No, I'm not pushing her away. But if I were, that is my choice to make."

"Of course it is," she says. "But that doesn't mean it would be the right choice." She lets that sink in and then says, "You think you're doing her a favor, but you're actually doing her a disservice. You're not allowing her to take an equal part in your relationship."

"And I'm supposed to take this advice from someone who has been single for more than a year? Maybe you should ask yourself why you're forever single instead."

Caitlyn's eyes fill with tears as she whips her head away and storms out.

You're a moron.

I know.

16

I slowly descend the staircase and look for any sign of Caitlyn. Suddenly, Kylie pops around from the corner.

"You're a dick," she pronounces.

"I'm aware," I reply. "Where is she?"

"She left to go 'grab some food,'" she says, "but I really think she left to get away from you."

"I see," I say meagerly.

"You embarrassed her," Kylie says, condemning.

"I know I did," I say, rubbing my forehead. "I don't know what's wrong with me."

"I think you should text her," she offers. "If you don't, I can't see her coming back tonight."

"I will," I say, grabbing my phone.

"And be honest."

"I know, I know."

"Was that attitude?"

"No, Kylie," I exhale loudly. "Sorry."

"That's better," she says, watching me intently as I text. "I shouldn't help you tonight with your little 'project,' but I'm still going to. I'll find you a loner to talk to. You certainly need someone to connect to in a positive way."

"Thank you, I really didn't mean…"

"But," she interrupts, "it's not gonna be another knock-out, sex kitten like last time. You need a reality check, brother."

"That's fair," I agree. "I never asked for a 'babe' to begin with, ya know."

Kylie looks me over. "You disgust me." With that, she walks away.

"Oh, come on, Kyle!" I shout. "Don't be like that. We're still friends."

"Still a jerk!" she hollers from the other side of the lobby.

She isn't wrong.

I stand behind the bar for the next thirty minutes. Technically, I am not supposed to serve alcohol at the theater since I am under twenty-one (that is strictly Ronnie and/or Margie's job), but what kind of narc is gonna sell me out when I am doing him a solid by selling him another brew to keep his buzz going for the climax of a movie? I flip one of our empty beer taps nonchalantly back and forth (the repetition of its clicking is somehow satisfying to me when I am in my head too much), when I see Kylie return to the lobby. Once she spots me, she heads my way.

"I heard you switched the line-up for tonight," she says.

"Yep."

"Why?"

"Caitlyn's suggestion."

Kylie's evaluation of me softens. "Well, she knows what she's doing. Probably a good choice. What did you decide on?"

"*Paper Moon* and *Birdman*."

"*Birdman*? Is that like a comic book thing?"

"Not exactly."

"What's the connection?"

"Don't you ever just want to watch the two movies and discover the connection for yourself, without someone else explaining it for you, word-for-word?"

Kylie looks me directly in the eyes and speaks soberly. "Guy, I am only asking you these questions because I am your… *reluctant* friend. I don't actually give a damn about any of these movies or film theory or mis-en-scene, or any of that other bullshit. I'm just trying to be nice and make you feel more important than you are."

I stare back. We are in some sort of duel, akin to a classic western showdown. Clearly, she has won this round. "Fair enough," I shoot. I look down in defeat and when I do, I notice something unusual. "What is on your shoes?"

"Oh, these?" she says with enthusiasm, completely moving on. "Air fresheners!"

Kylie has strapped an air freshener to each of her ankles so that the pine trees hang over her shoes. "Um… why?" I ask.

Kylie breaks out in the running-man dance on cue and sings, "So that everyone – knows – how – fresh – me – and – my – kicks – be!"

Something about Kylie's insanity always makes me feel better. "Did you change your hair again?"

"I did!" she flips it out with a hand. "Thanks for noticing uh-gin!" she says in her usual vapid, "influencer" voice. "If I didn't know better, I'd say you are a little too interested in what's going on in my life…" She throws her arm around me as she fake-chews gum.

"I like it," I say, ignoring the last part of her comment. "I don't think I've seen you with 'normal' hair for, like, years…"

"Normal?" she asks, dropping all enthusiasm. She looks hurt.

"Well, I didn't mean… I just meant…"

"This is platinum blonde!"

"I know…"

"I'm gonna have to change it again, or cut it or…"

"Kylie, come on. Settle down. It looks good. You're still completely unique."

"You think so?"

"I can say with all honesty that there is no one quite like you."

That's the crazy thing about Kylie. She is always so busy cutting and dying her hair to try and reach some level of beauty that seems out of reach for her, but if she just allowed herself to sit still for a moment, she could maybe see the effortless beauty that is inherent within her.

Coming off my compliment, she smiles and then abruptly fires into another thought, which is common for her. "Boy, do I have the perfect loner for you."

Kylie and I definitely each have a psychosis of some kind, but they are totally different kinds.

"Oh, yeah?" I say as I go back to tapping the empty draft tap back and forth.

"Yeah," she confirms. "And she's much different than the last one."

"A 'she,' eh?" I am thoroughly surprised.

"Yes, it's a woman, but this is a *real* woman," Kylie asserts. "Not like the last one. She was more of a walking male fantasy than a genuine person."

"I don't think that's very fair to Maya," I say, somewhat offended on her behalf.

"Well, *Maya* wasn't fair to the rest of us," Kylie spouts. Just then Caitlyn reemerges. She puts her coat on the rack and joins us. "I was just tellin' Guy here that I found his loner for the night," Kylie says.

"Oh, yeah?" Caitlyn adds, a bit disengaged.

I hesitate before I attempt a verbal apology. "Cate, I'm sorry…"

Caitlyn holds up a hand. "It's fine. Really. I just had a lot on my mind today."

"Like what?" I ask.

Caitlyn shrugs. "Maybe I'll fill you in later," she says. "What's this loner like, Kyle?"

"I don't want to ruin the surprise for Guy, so I think I'll hold on to that information for now," Kylie says. "So what's up, Cate? You good?"

Caitlyn gives a smirk that struggles upward. "Yeah, I'm good. Thanks."

An awkward silence falls over the three of us, which is very unusual. Normally we are all fighting to get the next word in. It is a bit disheartening that even *that* sensation seems to be falling away, too. Our chemistry, just like everything else in our lives, is fading.

Kylie looks at the clock in the lobby. "Welp, it's almost start time. We gonna go chill upstairs again? Roof time?"

It seems a shame not to use all the time the three of us have left together in a meaningful way. "Yeah, for sure," I say.

"Cool, and then we'll come back down for intermission. Are you good to approach the loner again, Cate?"

Caitlyn nods. "Sure thing. I'm always willing to help. Perhaps that's my fatal flaw."

Ouch. More to come on that, I can only assume.

17

Caitlyn, Kylie, and I pull ourselves up onto the roof again and assume our usual spots. *Same soup, just reheated.* I pull out my Red Bull, Kylie pulls out her speaker, and Caitlyn searches for music. Unlike last time, Kylie immediately takes out a joint and lighter. She is not looking for permission tonight and assures us of that when she catches Caitlyn and me looking at her.

"Remember," she says, mumbled, with the joint in her mouth, "you said you wouldn't give me grief this time. Right?" She doesn't even look at us as we reluctantly nod our heads. "That's what I thought," she mumbles again as she lights the joint. She takes a deep drag and then offers it to both of us. As usual, we both shake our heads no. Kylie exhales, surveys the stars, and takes another big drag.

"What are we listening to?" I say as I peer toward Caitlyn's phone.

"Remember, play somethin' trippy," Kylie says.

Caitlyn groans. "I don't have a lot of 'trippy' music like you do, Kyle."

"What's the trippiest thing you've listened to lately?" she asks.

Caitlyn thinks. "Mmm, I dunno... I heard a Bob Marley song in a cartoon I was watching the other day."

"Ugh," Kylie groans.

"Sorry I'm not into *Snoop* or *Kid Cudi* or *Tool* or freakin' *Jethro Tull*," Caitlyn scoffs.

"*Jethro Tull?*" I ask, astonished. All three of us laugh absurdly as if we have already caught a second-hand high.

"Why do you still smoke joints?" I ask Kylie after our laughter subsides.

"What do you mean?" she exhales in a coughing fit that matches one of Ronnie's.

"I mean, everyone vapes now... pens... and you still roll joints like Rooster Cogburn."

"I dunno," she considers. "I like the process of it. Feels more real to me. Like, it's not a fad or anything. I don't smoke for clout, like vapers do."

"Why do you smoke at all?" Caitlyn asks.

Kylie stares with red eyes up at the ever-intensifying and evolving sky. "Plenty of reasons."

Caitlyn lets that comment go, knowing that Kylie clearly is not ready to speak about whatever is on her mind.

I do not let it go, however. "You know, you can talk to us, Kylie. We wouldn't judge you or anything."

The rooftop falls quiet. Of course, such a quiet atmosphere instills paranoia in stoners, so Kylie takes another hit to ease her anxiety, which also, conversely, creates new and deeper anxieties. "I know that." She pauses. "Do you know what's interesting?"

"*A Love Supreme* by John Coltrane?" I suggest.

"What?" Caitlyn says.

"Never mind," I answer. "What, Kyle?"

"You're so worried about the future, Guy, but I envy you."

"Why would you envy me?"

"You think your future is uncertain, but why do you have to view it that way? I mean, you have a job. A secure job. A girlfriend. Friends. Ya know, *us*. Your parents care about you." Caitlyn and I remain quiet as Kylie tries to work out her thought process. She does not seem to notice. "Maybe what I'm saying is… what isn't good enough for you might be more than enough for someone else. Probably *anyone* else."

"I just don't like the uncertainty," I conclude slowly. "The idea of being alone."

"But you're not," she interjects.

"No, not right now. But soon. We all will be."

"That could be a good thing, though," Caitlyn quickly adds, picking up on the tension. "I mean, you are pretty excited to save up for your trip for Europe. Right, Kylie?"

Kylie takes another hit. "Thank you for acknowledging that my pipe dream is even a possibility."

I cannot be sure in the dark, but it seems as though Kylie has tears running down her face. *I thought weed was supposed to make you happy?* "Of course, it's a possibility," I add. "You're literally the most outgoing person I know. If you set your mind to something, I have no doubt you'll accomplish it."

Kylie chuckles. "Sorry, I don't mean to be the sad stoner girl. Usually this shit helps. Alcohol makes me emo, not this." She hesitates about what to say next, how to explain what is on her mind. "I appreciate you guys, even if your sentiments sound a bit cliché."

"Can I ask you something?" Caitlyn says.

"Sure," Kylie agrees.

"Why New York? Out of all of the places you could go after high school to earn money for your trip, why go there?"

"When I have an answer to that, I'll let you know." Kylie sits up. "Are you going to play a song or what?" She attempts to be her usual playful self, but we all know it is an act.

"Something trippy, right?" Caitlyn says.

"Trippy A-F," she agrees.

The subtle screams and guitar of Pink Floyd's "Breathe" begin. Kylie lies back down.

"Mr. Coen was playing this song before school today," Caitlyn says. "This okay?"

"It's perfect," Kylie agrees.

As the song begins, I gaze on the town below. For a rare moment, I find comfort. Once I find that solace, I ease back and take in the sky with my friends. Unlike our other nights on the roof, we do not attempt to play handball or cards or create viral videos. We just lie on the roof and take in the music – absorb it as one. We can all sense the change coming, and while none of us knows how to confront it, exactly, as high school seniors, we take a moment to just…

"Breathe, breathe in the air
Don't be afraid to care
Leave, but don't leave me
Look around
Choose your own ground
For long you live and high you fly
Smiles you'll give and tears you'll cry
All you touch and all you see
Is all your life will ever be"

18

As *Paper Moon* ends and as intermission approaches, Kylie leads Caitlyn into the theater auditorium to point out tonight's loner. I have maybe ten minutes before the (slight) rush of customers swarms the concession stand. I have never liked this feeling – the tension of knowing something is headed my way, there is nothing I can do to stop it, and I do not know enough of the specifics to prepare for it.

But that's the whole thing, isn't it? That is why I am stressing so much about the coming months and the changes they will bring. I do not like feeling out of control. Perhaps that is why I never indulged in drugs or alcohol, like Kylie so freely does. Life is scary enough without feeling even more absent-minded. I want to be prepared for anything, and I have never felt more unprepared in my life than I do right now.

I wish I had somebody to blame for this sensation. In truth, I know I cannot blame anyone else. I want nothing more than to be blissfully ignorant… to let life sweep me up and do with me what it will. My brain, however, is just not programmed that way. I have to overanalyze everything. I must self-deprecate. I am uneasy because I do not know what it means to be "at ease." I know I am not the only one who feels this way, but it sure feels like it in moments like these.

Moments before the rush.

"You're good to go, loser," Kylie announces as she and Caitlyn hop behind the concession counter to lend me a hand.

"How did it go?" I ask Caitlyn. "Was she weirded out? Or was she somehow cool with the whole thing, like Maya was? I honestly don't know which I prefer…"

"She was definitely weirded out, I'd say," Caitlyn admits. This development makes my stomach drop. I do not want to be a weirdo bothering people, after all. Caitlyn then says, "But once I explained the whole fake 'college essay' thing, she let her guard down and was cool with it."

"People must think that college has changed a lot over the years," Kylie shakes her head. "Like, what kind of university would require such amateurish investigative journalism as an intro requirement?"

"I think that most people don't remember much of their college years, and they don't want to admit it, so they willingly buy a story like this," I suggest.

"Right," Kylie nods. "It's better for the older generations to overlook the whole acid-trip thing, if they can, and pretend it was all about studying."

"Did your parents do LSD in college?" I ask. I realize that this conversation is, perhaps, not the most appropriate one to have at the moment only when I look up and notice an elderly woman slowly shaking her head at me. She quickly moves on.

I have got to learn to be more aware of my surroundings.

"My dad didn't," Kylie says. "He says drugs are for junkies and townies. The only thing worse than a drug-user, in his eyes, is someone who gets tattoos."

"Really?" Caitlyn asks.

"Yeah, he says they're all white trash," Kylie confirms. "So he never did any partying. But my mom was a huge stoner. Well, she was an overall drug-user."

"*Really?*" Caitlyn asks again.

"Oh, yeah," Kylie nods. "She told me she used to wake and bake before class every morning in college. The problem was that after a while, she started to get more and more paranoid after she did it. So she would smoke a joint and then go into the bathroom, ride the high out in the bath tub, and then come out two hours later when she was leveling out."

"How did she pass her classes?" I ask.

"Oh, she didn't," Kylie acknowledges with a stoner's chuckle. I find it quite ironic that Kylie is giving us the rundown on her mother's drug history while Kylie herself is still high. "She stopped going to classes because of the whole morning bathroom routine. And that was just the weed. She'd eat mushrooms once every month or so, on top of everything else. You know, snort coke in bar restrooms on the weekends, drop acid during concerts, pop downers to fall asleep at night. When you add booze to all of that, too, just to socialize and be like everyone else… man, it wasn't long before she completely failed out of college."

"Holy crap," Caitlyn says. "I can't believe she told you all of that. I think my parents would be too embarrassed to ever mention they even *tried* drugs."

"Well, I think she told me as a scare tactic," Kylie ponders. "You know, to scare me straight. Hoping that I wouldn't go down the same road as her."

Caitlyn and I say nothing, but I know we are thinking the exact same thing. How can we not? Kylie's eyes are as red as the ember at the end of her recently lit joint. I allow the last customer to exit the line before I continue the conversation. I begin to speak, but Caitlyn, surprisingly, beats me to my point.

"Don't you feel bad?" she asks slowly.

"What do you mean?" Kylie replies.

"You know… about drinking and smoking," Caitlyn nearly whispers. "Don't you worry about…?"

"Ending up like her?" Kylie asks. "Yeah, I do. But I dunno, I still do it. I'm not getting carried away."

"But if you're parent is an addict…" Caitlyn continues, "… I mean, that stuff is hereditary, ya know?" I am glad Caitlyn is asking these questions and not me. Yes, I too am curious about Kylie's answers, but I do not feel brave enough to psychoanalyze her. Caitlyn then adds, "Don't you feel like you're kinda… disrespecting her in a way?"

And then Kylie does something she never does – falls silent. She begins to speak, but it is jumbled and confused. "No, no, it's not like that. I mean, I know my limitations. I don't want to be like that either." She then pauses again, more than likely feeling judged. "I mean, we can't all be perfect like you, Caitlyn."

"I'm far from perfect, and I'm pretty sure you know that," she replies.

The tension within our group is high again (an uncomfortable developing trend), but this time around, I am not to blame. I keep my mouth shut to keep it that way.

"You're right," Kylie says softly. "I'm sorry. I just… ya know… I don't know."

"I know," Caitlyn acknowledges.

Nothing direct is said in the moment, but we all come to a mutual understanding that could have not been more clear – *life is complicated, man.*

"What about your parents, Guy?" Caitlyn asks. "Were they potheads?"

"Well, Guy's parents were in college in the thirties, most likely, so I don't think pot was invented yet," Kylie laughs.

"Oh, I think it was invented," Caitlyn laughs, "but according to movies, only jazz musicians did it back then. Ya know, they'd burn a reefer in between sets."

"*Reefer*?" Kylie laughs.

"Well, what should I call it? Weed is used too much, and so is pot and grass."

"How about ganja?" I offer.

"The herb," Kylie adds.

"Mary Jane," Caitlyn says.

"The chronic."

"Nugget."

"Fatty boom blatty."

"Combustible herbage."

"Wacky tobaccy."

"The devil's cabbage," Caitlyn tops us all off as we cackle.

"Yeah, no way," Kylie brings the conversation back. "Guy's parents were probably bootlegging moonshine and hanging out in speakeasys, amirite?"

I cannot help but laugh. "Yeah, I think my parents were a little ahead of the whole counter-culture drug thing. I can't see either of them burning a 'j.'" Our mirth continues.

The idea of my parents getting high is as foreign to me as the power of the Soviet Union. "So back to the matter at hand," I continue, "I'm good to go after the next movie?"

"You're good to go," Caitlyn confirms.

"Thank you," I say sincerely.

"What's the loner's name?" Kylie asks. "Did you get to feel her out any?"

"I got to know a little about her, once she realized I wasn't a threat," Caitlyn says.

"You're probably the least-threatening person of all time," I say. "I can't believe she couldn't spot that right away."

"She sounds a bit skittish," Kylie agrees. "Like someone who watches the twenty-four hour cable news cycle without ever leaving the house."

"You're not wrong," Caitlyn kind of agrees. "She seemed very nice, though. But yes, there is something about her that feels… skeptical."

"What did you find out exactly?" Kylie asks.

"She lives alone…" Caitlyn begins.

"Shocking," Kylie interrupts.

"…and she is unmarried with no kids," Caitlyn continues. "She looked like she was about forty to forty-five years old."

"She's truly a loner," I say. I do not mean it as an insult, although it inevitably sounds like one. I am just stating the fact – a fact that I need to become comfortable with myself. "And what is her name?"

"Her name is Lauren."

19

From the doorway, I can hear the sound of *Birdman* finally coming to an end. Part of me wishes I had watched the movie tonight, even though I have already seen it numerous times. I just love it, despite the maybe less-than-stellar ending. *Who cares?* The ending is not the most important thing, after all. *Right?* It is supposed to be about the journey.

The film that played first, *Paper Moon*, does end remarkably. It is one of the best things about the film in general. Everything crumbles down around the young girl and her father (?), but it's okay because they have each other, and that is all they need. It is a strange mixture of both a happy and unhappy ending.

I was so quick to change the movie selection tonight after Caitlyn suggested it. I wonder why that was. I think I just take her advice so highly. She is well put-together in every conceivable way; I just assume she always knows what is best.

As I think of *Paper Moon*'s ending, I cannot help but think of the ending of *Whiplash*, the film I originally planned to screen instead of *Birdman*. *Whiplash*'s ending is my favorite of all time. It would have been so fitting for it to play in this moment, too.

What does it mean?

Did Andrew succeed?

Was Fletcher correct in his methods? The whole time?

Does being successful in your passions trump everything else?

These are questions I think about every time I think about *Whiplash*, and while they always go unanswered, I still find comfort in them, because asking those questions is just as important as getting answers.

Maybe that is why I get stuck on the endings of movies, whether it is *Birdman*, *Paper Moon*, or *Whiplash*. I hate not knowing an outcome – just like everyone else does – but I also think that not knowing a definitive answer can be just as rewarding. Sometimes it is good to not have everything spelled out for you, as I advised Kylie earlier. I have always maintained that.

The ending is not the most important thing – it is the journey.

As the audience files out of the theater, I spot my next loner still within. While still seated, she looks around nervously, almost awaiting some great prank or scam to be played upon her. I approach her slowly, cautiously.

"Lauren?" I inquire.

She jerks her head toward me and offers a forced smile. "Yes?"

"Hey, I'm Guy," I say, extending my hand. She shakes it as I continue. "I believe you met my coworker already – Caitlyn?"

"Oh, yes," she nods, visibly becoming more comfortable. "She's such a sweet girl."

"The best," I agree.

"She was telling me that you needed to interview several people for a college project?" she asks as I nod. "I'm just not sure what I can offer you in terms of information. I didn't attend college myself."

"Oh, that's not a necessity," I clarify. "I just need to interview people of all kinds. Sort of like a human interest thing."

"I see."

I can tell Lauren is still reluctant to buy what I am trying to sell. "I could start off with an easy question, to give you an idea of what the overall interview will be like, if you'd prefer?"

"Okay."

Lauren's increasingly short responses alert me to the fact that she is growing more and more skeptical of me (and my lies).

"Are you a life-long resident of this area?" I ask.

"Yes, I am."

"So you graduated high school here? In Hudson?"

"Yes."

"Did you go to a trade school, or did you enter the work force straight out of high school?"

"I went to work."

"What kind of work did you do?"

She shifts in her seat. "Does it matter?"

Lauren is clearly not going to be the easy interview that Maya was. I simply had to ask Maya her name and before I knew it, she was telling me about banging an older dude on top of his office desk. Lauren, I get the feeling, is a little more old-fashioned in what she will reveal.

"I'm sorry, I don't mean to pry. I simply like to ask these questions to get a feel of what opportunities were available to those in this area after high school."

That explanation seems to calm Lauren's nerves. She no longer expects me to steal her Social Security number, I reckon. "No, I'm sorry. I just get kinda anxious talking about myself. I worked in retail after high school. I slowly made my way up to supervisor over the years. That's what I do now."

"Okay, great. Thank you," I jot some phony notes down in my notebook. "What made you want to go into retail?"

"I don't think anyone *wants* to go into retail," she asserts

"No?"

"No. It was simply my only option at the time. And once I was in… that was it. Like a black hole you can't get unstuck from, especially if you were a woman at that time with only a high school diploma."

"I see," I scribble some more. "Did your parents encourage you to further your education, or were they just happy you were making money right away?"

After finally unlocking the safe that is Lauren's willingness, it suddenly closes again after that question. I can tell I upset her, but I am not sure why.

"I'm sorry, we can move on…"

"My mother didn't encourage further education because we didn't have that luxury. She was working two jobs minimum at the time, so money was our priority."

"What about…? Or did…?"

"My father?" she pauses. "My father didn't encourage anything from me except a feeling of longing."

A heavy air cloaks us. Clearly this is why Lauren is a closed book and why she attends movies alone. Everyone has a reason, but some are more sinister than others.

"We can move on."

"You don't want to know about him?"

"Sure, I do, but I don't…"

"Listen, if you want to know why my life is the way it is, then that's where it begins."

20

"My father was a raging alcoholic," Lauren begins. "And I mean *raging*. Some people claim that there is such a thing as a 'functioning' alcoholic, but I never witnessed that. It was all or nothing with him. If there were twelve beers in the house at the beginning of the night, they were gone by morning. If there were forty beers and two fifths of whiskey at the beginning of the night, then they were gone by morning. Whatever was on hand, he consumed – every night. There were no breaks or exceptions."

I try to digest Lauren's story without any sort of judgement. Clearly there is a lot to unpack here, but I am not a therapist – I am a high school senior. *What help can I possibly offer this woman?*

"Was he always that way?" I ask meagerly.

"For as long as I can remember," she says tersely. "With *one* exception. But he left when I was six years old."

"Where did he go?"

"North."

"Like the Dakotas or Canada?"

"No, like thirty miles north. Still in Missouri."

"Oh, wow."

"Yeah."

"So what did he do there? Were you under shared custody or…?"

"No, he never interacted with me again. He started a new family. We were just a trial run, I guess."

"He started a new family? Just like that? And so close?"

"It wasn't like it is today. Back then, you could up and leave your family and never see them again, even if you were within commuting distance. We didn't have cell phones or the internet. You could begin a new life pretty easily."

This development astounds me. "How did you find out about his new family?"

"My mom discovered them, years later, I think. I must have been twelve or thirteen. My mom never drank after he left us, but she got really depressed when her mother died."

"I'm sorry."

"When Grandma died, my mom basically fell apart. She had lost, basically, the last person she could depend upon for guidance or help. So after she passed away, my mom had a moment of weakness. I can still remember the night. I got home from school and the house was empty, which was not unusual. It was always empty. Like I said, my mom worked several jobs, so she was gone more often than not."

"I'm sorry."

Lauren pauses. "Well, you don't have to be sorry, kid. Relax."

I smile for the first and, most likely, last time during her story. Little levity seems to be likely in Lauren's life story. "Sorry," I say, chuckling. She joins me.

"Anyway, the day grew dark, and there was still no sign of Mom. I went ahead and cooked a simple dinner for myself – something else I was accustomed to – and ate it in front of the TV. Just when I was ready to head to bed after my shower, my mom came bursting through the door, a drunk, sobbing mess. It shocked me. I was used to seeing my dad furiously drunk, even when I was a small child, but never my mom. Are your parents drinkers?"

"No, not really. They certainly never get drunk around me. Just a glass of wine here and there."

"Consider yourself lucky. There is something very disarming about seeing a parent out of control. It may sound extreme, but it shakes the foundation of your life. Here is this person who is supposed to protect you in every way, and all of a sudden, it feels as though you're unsafe in every way, including from them."

"I can't imagine."

"But it was that night she told me about Dad. What she had discovered about him. He had moved on, started new, and was living his best life. She was angry when she began the story, throwing things and screaming, but by the time she had finished, she collapsed into me, sobbing and asking me to hold her. Our roles in the family reversed. It was the most horrific night of my life."

"You were only twelve. Of course it was."

Suddenly, Lauren's inner defenses seem to lock into place again. "I'm sorry, I shouldn't unload all of this onto you. You're just a kid."

"You don't have to be sorry," I say. "Relax."

She gives me a knowing smile. "I don't get asked many questions about my life, as you can probably tell."

"Especially about that part of it, I would imagine."

"No," she agrees.

"What was your mom like? Other than that night?"

"She was harsh, but she had to be, in many ways. After Dad left, she was pulled in every direction and in every way. She had to be provide a home and guidance for me. She needed to be a good employee to her bosses, never letting on that she was too tired to complete one work shift, let alone two or three consecutive shifts. Her sense of self was completely lost after that. She had no more personal life."

"Sounds stressful, to you and her both."

"Do you know how a person acts under that kind of pressure?"

"I have a feeling…"

"Because she was so overworked, she became a tyrant at home. She kept me firmly under her thumb. Her punishments were never anything but strict, and they were handed out readily. Often, she would lash out at me when everything seemed fine. It was hard to tell what could set her off. Sometimes it was as simple as something I cooked or the smell of the air on certain summer nights. She endured a lot of trauma herself, after all."

"Did you become rebellious after your father left? Maybe that's why…?"

"No, I honestly didn't. I toed the line at home, and everywhere else, because I didn't want to upset her. I was afraid of her"

"Because she would hit you?"

"Oh, yeah, all the time. That's not even what I'm talking about, though."

"Then what were you afraid of?"

Lauren pauses for the first time in a long time. "I was afraid that if I upset her too much, then she would leave, too."

The emptiness of the theater amplifies the sensation we feel. I am not sure what to say. *What can I say? I don't have any life experience to make her feel better about what she just said... the truth she revealed.*

"You don't have to say anything," Lauren says, as if picking up on my uneasiness. "I am the way that I am because I am a product of the environment my parents created for me, just like everyone else."

"But you seem so..." I begin to say hesitantly.

"So what?"

"I dunno, like nice. Normal. From the outside, I mean."

"Those of us who are damaged, or have been hurt, become great actors. We are great at hiding our defects, because we have to. The defects makes those around us feel uncomfortable, and that's the last thing damaged people want. We don't want to re-create environments that resemble the very thing we are running away from. We want everyone around us to feel... *okay*."

"That makes a lot of sense," I agree. "Surely there were some good moments, though. Right? I would hate to believe that a person's life could be so unrelentingly sad."

"There was one good moment. I mentioned it earlier."

"I don't recall."

"Well, I said I can only remember spending one day with my father when he was completely sober. I was so young, but it is one of my most vivid memories."

"What happened? What were you guys doing?"

"We went to the movies."

And now it all makes sense.

21

"My memory begins in the car. I was in the backseat, so happy to be going on a journey with both of my parents. I can still remember how unhappy I was as a child. My house was full of tension. But that's what made that day so great. There was no tension in the car. My parents were *finally* getting along for once. They were laughing together and singing along to songs on the radio. It was as if I got a small glimpse into the chemistry that allowed the two of them to even fall in love with each other in the first place. Not only that, but I finally got to feel what other normal, 'happy' families were like. The ones I saw around me everywhere, or so it seemed. But it always seems that way, I suppose, when you're from such a dysfunctional and unhappy family.

"When we got to the theater, I sprinted to the box office. I eagerly waited for my parents to join up at the ticket booth, where I was grinning ear to ear. After getting our tickets, we walked into the lobby and I was blown away. It was a special trip that had taken us to a multiplex in North Kansas City. I had never been to such a big theater in my life. It seemed so out of this world. Literally. The ceiling was covered with painted stars and glorious constellations. Being so young, I really felt as though I were looking into another galaxy.

"The only thing that mesmerized me more than the massive ceiling mural was the smell of the place. As soon as we walked through the lobby doors, the smell of buttery popcorn smashed into my nose like an unexpected snowball. While completely satisfied the moment before, I grew instantly and furiously hungry. My parents, being in such great moods, visited the concession stand next, which had also never happened before.

"We entered our screening room and found seats toward the back and on the aisle. I sat between my parents, but that didn't stop their frequent moments of affection. My dad put his arm around my mom and pulled her close, which in turn pulled the two of them right over the top of my head. I didn't mind, though. They even snuck in a few kisses over my head throughout the movie. Before the movie started, though, my father, who was never one to be overly touchy-feely with his affection, pulled me in under his arm. I never felt more at ease in my life – before or since.

"Once the previews began, I entered another world – a world free from fighting, screaming, cursing, smoking, drinking, throwing, or hitting. It was free of the tension that my house had absorbed and allowed to grow like some sort of infectious botfly. I already knew it was the best day of my life before the movie even began.

"The movie we saw was *The Jerk*, starring Steve Martin. Not your typical family fare, but my family was not typical. My parents – and probably more so my father – wanted to see that movie, so that was that. There was no thought given to the fact that their six-year-old daughter was going to watch the R-rated film with them or that I wouldn't understand the humor. But it was okay. I didn't need to understand the movie to enjoy it. I enjoyed it because they did. The three of us shared ninety minutes of laughter and joy.

"After the movie, we went to a Chili's restaurant. Dinner went just as well as the movie. I was allowed to order whatever I wanted, disregarding the usual restrictions (only kids meals and no soda). The joyful behavior was so complete that I never expected it to end. Why should it? Why should things suddenly revert to the past once we got into our car? Or once we arrived at our house? Or once we woke up the next morning? It never had to change because that day didn't have to be an outlier. We could allow happiness in our home if we allowed it. If we encouraged it. It felt good to all three of us, after all.

"We didn't make it until the next day, though. We didn't even make it to the car. I can remember feeling the tension, the stomach-turning sensation that children often feel when something's wrong with their parents, once the check arrived at dinner. After that moment, for whatever reason, my parents went back to their usual selves. By the time we were driving home, they were screaming at each other as if the perfect day hadn't just existed."

"When did your dad leave?" I ask slowly. I am not sure what is appropriate to ask in this moment, but it is the only question I can think to ask. I am so engrossed in her words that the idea of tactfulness escapes me.

"He left probably a month later, from what I can recall," Lauren thinks aloud, with one eye shut as she recalls the time. "That theater visit is the last happy memory I have of my parents. It was the *only* happy memory I was able to create for many, many years. It took probably a decade for me to re-define what being 'happy' or 'normal' meant."

"I know you're going to tell me not to be 'sorry,' but I can't help my need to say it," I offer.

"I understand," she chuckles. "What are you gonna do? Life's not fair to everyone."

"It should be, though," I mutter. "Is that why…?" I begin to ask, noticing her proximity to the screen – back row, right side, and on the aisle.

"Why I'm here tonight?" she smiles. "Yeah. I come as often as I can, whether I have anyone with me or not. Movie theaters have always felt more like home to me than any house I've lived in. It was in a theater that I felt the idea of home – the closeness of familial love. That never happened anywhere else. I chase that feeling like a drug every weekend."

"Did you ever find that feeling again?"

Lauren turns away from me instantly, emotion hitting her face like that popcorn smell did so many years ago. "No, but that never stopped me from trying."

22

"Enough of my sob story," Lauren says, composing herself. "What about your parents? I hope they don't compare to mine."

I offer an uneasy chuckle. "No, not that I would be super happy about bragging on my home life to you, but no, they were good parents."

"Were?" Lauren asks.

"Sorry, they *are* good parents," I clarify. "My bad." Lauren's brow furrows after my simple mistake. "What?"

"It's just weird," she says. "Both of my parents are dead, and I still refer to them in the present tense. Both of your parents are alive, and yet you spoke of them in the past tense. I wonder why that is?"

"I just misspoke," I shrug.

"Are you close to your parents?" she asks.

"As close as any kid can be I guess," I answer. *Well, that was kinda dumb to say now that I think about it.*

"Maybe you used the past tense because you're subconsciously prepping yourself for when you have to leave home after graduation," she suggests.

I do not even have to think over my reply. "No, that's not it. First off, I'm not leaving after graduation. Secondly, I have always been prepared to be on my own. My subconscious has become conscious in that regard."

"Why is that? Why have you *always* been prepared to be on your own?"

Lauren was right. It is difficult to answer questions about my family in theory, but in the moment, when I am asked directly, I find myself unable to stop. Maybe it is because no one has taken the time to ask about my parents' relationship with me and I have not had time to come up with prepared answers. Or maybe it is because I have been needing to talk about that particular relationship, and once I see my moment, my guard completely drops. Whatever the reason, I feel comfortable talking to Lauren about my parents. How could I not, after everything she has told me?

"My parents are old," I begin.

"Everyone's parents are old," she interrupts. "That's how it goes. And they seem even older to you when you're a kid."

"No, I mean my parents are like *old* old," I explain. "When my mom had me, it was called a geriatric pregnancy."

"How old are they?"

"Late sixties."

"Wow, that is old. I mean, to have a senior in high school."

I can tell that Lauren is now the one afraid of offending me. I laugh to ease her conscience. "No, it's okay. Everyone knows it's kind of a preposterous situation. I'm used to it. I've heard all of the jokes."

"Do you have any brothers or sisters?"

"Nope. I'm an only child."

"I guess that would make you prepared for anything," she says. "Still, even given your current circumstance, why aren't you leaving after high school? To go to college or find a new town to live in or whatever? Most kids are excited to do that."

"When the time comes, this theater is my inheritance," I explain. "And since this theater is all but dying in the moment, I have a significant reason to try and keep it alive. That's why I try to be innovative about our movie selections and events. I'll do anything to attract customers."

"It seems like you like it here, though. Maybe it's not all bad that you aren't leaving after high school."

"That's the thing, though," I exhale. "I honestly wish I could leave. My girlfriend is moving to another city, my friends are all leaving… I want to leave, but I can't."

"Why don't you ask your parents about the prospect of selling the property then?"

"I can't do that."

"Why not? If it's your inheritance, you should have a little say in it."

"I can't do that because this theater is their legacy. This is how the community will remember them. And once they're gone, this will be how I remember them, too. Every day when I walk in here, I feel like I'm stepping into my home. Kind of like how you feel. But it's an even stronger sensation for me because I spend more time here than I do at my actual home. I eat and even sleep here at times. We hold family dinners at the holidays here. I can smell my parents' aromas in every room and section. I can see their past actions when I round every corner. I can't give that up. I know that one day, I will be alone and I won't have anyone. No siblings or cousins… maybe not even a girlfriend or wife. I won't have anything, except this old theater. But on those days, when I know I'll feel alone, I also know that I'll be able to come here and still feel my parents' presence. I can't just allow some other family to move in here and take all that away. Pretend that all of this didn't happen. That they didn't... I don't have anything else. I can't allow their names or memories to disappear along with this theater."

I inhale sharply after my sudden exposition. It feels like I unveiled years of suppressed thoughts that I had denied acknowledging even to myself. I avoid looking directly at Lauren's eyes – avoid accepting any sort of judgment. I should know better, though.

"Your parents won't disappear with this theater, Guy," she says calmly. "We all have fears of abandonment – trust me. But as long as you strive to remember them, you will."

"It sounds kinda cliché, but it's true, isn't it?"

"It really is."

"Do you still strive to remember your parents, despite all the bad?"

"Yeah, I do. They're all I had, so in a way, I've never known the feeling of needing to expect more out of a parental figure. I mean, my mom was my better parent, and she still lashed out at me in fits of rage."

"I'm lucky, I guess."

"You really are. You don't realize how many people would kill to have your 'normal, boring' life."

"I'm gonna miss them," I say suddenly, seemingly out of nowhere.

"Hey," Lauren says, placing her hand on mine. "They aren't going anywhere yet."

"I know, but I can't help but think..."

"Guy."

"When they're gone, I really won't have anyone. They've been my whole life, really. They raised me, gave me a job, gave me a future... I don't know a life without them."

"No one knows a life without a parent, or parental figure. We all have that in common, and yet that doesn't make it any less terrifying. We all have to come to terms with being the 'elder' family member, and no one's ever ready for it."

"What was the hardest thing about losing your mom?" I ask.

"I couldn't ask her questions anymore," Lauren says. "About all sorts of things. Things you take for granted. Like where to get an oil change when your normal mechanic retires. Or how to file your taxes. Or how to start planning for retirement. Or how to buy a burial plot. All sorts of everyday things. But then there are the big questions, too. Like, 'What was Grandma like?' 'Would she have been proud of me?' 'What should I do when I suddenly start to question my faith?' 'What was your life with Dad like before you had me?' 'What drove him to drink?'" She pauses after that one, and then, "'Why wasn't I enough to make him stay?'"

She is right. I do not know how I will be able to function without my parents' guidance. It does not seem fair – especially when my parents' time is, inevitably, much more finite.

Outside of my own "high school" problems, however, I can still see that other people have it much worse than I do – people like Lauren. I never had to question why one of my parents left. Or if they loved me to begin with. *That* is unfair.

Never again let me take that for granted.

Suddenly, a head peeks in the doorway behind us. "Guy? You still in here?"

It is Caitlyn. "Yeah, I'm still here," I reply.

And just like that, Lauren stands and gathers her things as if the last half an hour did not happen. I think she is embarrassed she divulged so much. She seems to live a life of shame and regret, and all I want is to tell her that she does not have to. But who am I? An eighteen-year-old imbecile with no life experience. I am sure I would be a lot of help.

"You don't have to go so quickly," I tell her. "I'm closing the theater tonight, so there's no rush."

She frantically continues to put on her coat. "No, no, no. I've stayed long enough. I'm sure you have plenty to write something for your college thing," she says.

I know I am supposed to be ending my conversation with her, but I do not want it to end. Yes, I learned a lot from the last loner Maya, but I spent half of my time with her simply being titillated. With Lauren, I tuned into thoughts and fears I never knew I had about my future and my worries about my parents. Yes, she is a middle-aged loner, unassuming in every way imaginable, but she has opened my eyes.

"You're right," I answer her. "I do. Thank you."

Lauren stands still, finally, and looks me in the eyes. I know it is difficult for an introvert like her to do, but she does. "You're going to be okay, Guy."

With that, she smiles and walks away.

I really hope so.

23

"You were in there a long time," Caitlyn greets me as I enter the lobby. "I didn't expect you to spend so much time with her. I can understand why you wanted to linger with Maya..."

"I'm sorry, Cate," I interrupt her.

She stops and drops the forced niceties. That is the thing about Caitlyn. Even if she is mad at you, she will pretend she is not, just so you do not have to feel bad. She is a special kind of person, and I treated her like garbage before.

"It's really okay, Guy," she begins.

"But it's not," I assert. "You didn't deserve that. And despite my rudeness, you still helped me out tonight. Why?"

Caitlyn doesn't even hesitate. "Because you needed me. That's what friends do. I know you've been struggling."

"Why haven't you?" I ask her. "You're going through the same type of transitional period, and yet you haven't shown any nervousness. Why is that?'

"I'm not allowing myself to think that way," she says. "I know what I need to do to be successful, so I'm doing it. If I overthink it, then I'll just freak myself out. It doesn't change anything anyway, so why bother? I'll just push through like I always have."

"Your parents must be so proud of you," I chuckle. She laughs as well, waving me off. "No, I'm serious. You've always been an amazing student, athlete, and club leader. You never get into trouble, and you're one of the few people in our class who hasn't gotten black-out drunk or tried drugs. It's pretty impressive."

"I don't see why it's so hard to avoid making bad choices," she says, bemused. "Seriously. Look at everyone around us who has thrown their life away. People in the class above us... five years older than us... *the townies*. When I see them, I don't regret my decisions at all. In fact, I think it's easier to make good choices."

"You may be right," I say, somewhat astonished.

"Immediate gratification over long-term success? That's not even a question."

"Still, it's gotta be annoying to be constantly mocked for your 'goody-goody' decisions."

"Oh, it is, but I can't help that. It makes people feel better to bring someone else down. Everyone else in class thinks that I act superior to them, but that's not the case. Try being successful while also trying to fit in with everyone else. It's much more difficult than you'd think."

"Everyone has their own trials," I murmur.

"Is that what Lauren taught you tonight?" Caitlyn asks.

"Not in those words exactly, but yeah, that's what I'm learning."

"No one has it figured out, do they?"

"Have what figured out?"

"Life."

"No. No one does."

PART FOUR

CASABLANCA

LA LA LAND

24

"There are gonna be so many old people here tonight, it's not even funny."

Kylie has a way of really rallying up the morale before our work shifts. "Why do you say that?" I ask. "Why should tonight's double be any different, crowd-wise?"

"Because you chose an old-ass movie, *uh-gen*..."

"That's kinda the point."

"... and not only that, but you followed it up with a musical," she finishes. "No one likes musicals besides old people. And theater freaks, like my creepy cousins. You've met 'em. They come over at Thanksgiving and never say a word until we are all eating at the table. And then suddenly, they stand up, burst out into a song, and then walk away, complaining about how we are all 'ignorant' and not 'woke' enough. I just know that's how I am going to die one day... One of my cousins is going to incorporate my murder into a holiday song-and-dance number."

"That's kinda harsh," Caitlyn adds.

"Easy for you to say, Cate," Kylie continues. "You're not even scheduled to work tonight."

"Yeah, what are you doing here anyway?" I act offended.

"Is it not okay to check in on my friends?" she asks.

"Not when you have to go to your workplace to do it," Kylie answers. "I would never come here on my day off."

"How lame would that be?" I ask sarcastically, knowing that I basically live here. "What are you doing tonight anyway?"

"I think I'm gonna go to a movie with Sam and Christine," she answers.

"Wait a minute," I say, but Kylie quickly beats me to the obvious next question.

"You're going to a movie on your day off from working... *at a movie theater*?!" she nearly screams.

"Yeah, well, we're going to the city. You know, the nice theater up there?"

"Oh, well, thanks." I cannot help but be offended at the slight aimed at my second home.

"The Bristol is nice, too, but that one up there has the big, leather seats that recline and warm..." Caitlyn says in anticipated ecstasy.

This is why you're gonna fail, Guy... No one wants the traditional experience...

"You know, I used to always think Guy was the biggest loser in our group..."

"Hey!"

"But you have surpassed him today, Cate."

"Whatever," she says, brushing it off. "I don't question every aspect of your life."

"Yes, you do."

"No, I don't."

"Um, yes... *you do*."

"Like when?"

"Like anytime I want to party."

"Well..."

"Well...?"

"Well, that is kinda a bad choice on your part."

Kylie exhales in frustration. "This sucks. If I had the night off, I can assure you that I wouldn't go somewhere else where I felt like I was still working. You're even doing it now! You're literally hanging out at work!"

"Where would you go instead?" Caitlyn asks. Kylie does not immediately answer, so Caitlyn asks again, "Well?"

"Well, yeah, I'd go to a party," she answers.

"See?!" Caitlyn shouts. "So predictable."

"That's what we're supposed to do, *Cate*," Kylie informs her. "Enjoy our youth... take advantage of it... explore new situations... and people. Before long, all of these fun things are snatched away from us. But none of that matters anyway, because I'm stuck here tonight with Guy and the cast of *The Mule*."

By this point, Kylie is actually irritating me. "Do you really want the night off?" I ask sternly.

"Yes, I really do."

"Then go. Take it off. Ronnie and Margie will be here any minute. We can handle the crowd. Like you said, they're all ancient, so the three of us will be able to handle the senior 'rush' at intermission."

Kylie looks me over in a too-good-to-be-true fashion. "You serious, Guy?"

"I seriously don't want to hear you bitch tonight."

"Woah!" Kylie and Caitlyn both shout.

"What?" I ask.

"You can't say that," Caitlyn informs me.

"Yeah, Mr. Chauvinist. Who do you think you are?" Kylie asks.

"Relax. I wasn't calling you that. I was using 'bitch' in the verb tense."

Kylie and Caitlyn look at each other, evaluating my reasoning and potential punishment. Finally, Caitlyn nods. "Okay, but that's a warning."

"Oh, I'm so scared," I wiggle my fingers.

"You think they'll cover for me?" Kylie asks.

"Ronnie and Margie have no idea what's going on during a normal shift. They'll be just fine."

Kylie shrugs and nearly leaps for her coat. "Sounds good to me!"

Caitlyn grabs her coat as well and walks toward the door. "Oh, you're both leaving now?" I ask softly.

"You didn't seem to care a minute ago when you called us both bitches," Kylie scoffs.

"Enough," I say as I drop my head. "You're so exhausting."

"Ronnie and Margie are both walking up now," Caitlyn says as she peers out the open door. "You're covered," she says to Kylie.

"Okay," I concede. "Well, have fun guys."

"Someone else is with 'em, too," Caitlyn says, still peering out the door.

"Oh, yeah? Who?" I ask.

"Your parents."

25

Why are my parents here?!

I love my parents, but when they show up at the theater, while I am working, I always feel added pressure. *Make sure you're nice to the customers. Make sure you offer concessions. Make sure you scoop the popcorn from the bottom. Make sure you don't say anything bad about the movie they're about to see. Make sure you do us, and the theater, proud...*

"Hey, guys," I greet them as they walk in behind Ronnie and Margie. "What are you doing here tonight?"

"We thought we'd watch the movie," my mom answers, "and see how *you* are doing, of course."

"We love *Casablanca*," my dad agrees. "Doing okay tonight so far?"

"Yeah, we've had some people trickling in already," I answer.

"No, not the crowd," Dad clarifies. "I mean, *you*. Are you doing okay?"

"Me? Oh, yeah. I'm good. Everything's good here."

Dad smiles at me in that way that says, *I'm really proud of you, but I won't say it out loud so I don't embarrass you in front of strangers.*

I appreciate both his affection and concern towards me, but he is right. I do not like voicing such things out loud. It is a weird thing. I love my parents more than anything, or anyone, but I am always so hesitant to say that to them in person. I can even tell my friends and coworkers how much I think of my parents, but once they are in my vicinity, I shut down.

Why is that, Guy? Why do you have trouble telling those who are important to you how much you love them?

I don't know. That's what I'm trying to figure out.

Your parents… Brianna…

I know!

So instead of saying, "Hey, guys, it's great to see you! I missed and love you both so much!" I always go for comments that bust their chops or question their decision making. It seems rude or uncaring, but that is not it at all. In fact, I think I get somewhat uncomfortable around my parents because I *do* understand the gravity of what it is that they have done for me.

My parents created me. My mother went through an insanely intense labor to birth me. My father stayed up nights with me when he had to go to work early the next day. My mother has made me nearly every meal I have ever eaten. My father introduced me to sports and played outside with me every day. My mother gave me my sense of humor. My father gave me my understanding for respect and responsibility. They both sacrificed for me. They both shaped their *entire* lives around raising me – a child they had not even planned for.

How can I ever pay them back for that? How can I even begin to acknowledge all that they have done for me? Perhaps, it would be to say "I love you" at every possible moment. Yet, I am unable to do so, because it feels so inadequate.

"Are you staying for both movies?" I ask them. I am curious to know just how late my elderly parents are willing to stay up, but I am also wondering if they are going to be around when I interview my loner tonight. That may be hard to explain.

"We'll see how it goes, but I doubt it," Mom says.

"Well, can I get you guys anything?"

"I don't think so," Dad says. "It's too late to begin drinking soda."

"He'll be up all night," Mom agrees. "Five or six times, probably. And that wakes *me* up."

"Actually, yeah," Dad says, "get me a small popcorn, Guy."

"No, Richard," Mom interrupts.

"No, *what*?" Dad is taken off guard, but he should not be.

"Popcorn will just agitate your diverticulitis," Mom explains something he certainly already knows.

"Just a *small* bag," he says, holding up two fingers three inches apart. "A small bag won't do anything."

"Oh, no," she mocks him, "you certainly won't be holding your stomach all night, wondering where the sudden pain came from. Compared to popcorn, drinking soda late at night is nothing. You'll *really* be up all night if you eat popcorn."

"Carol…"

"Richard."

"*Carol.*"

I have noticed a weird thing about married-couple arguments. When the fight plateaus out – when there is nothing more to add or counterargue – the argument basically concludes with two people saying each other's names over and over again, until one of them finally breaks.

"*Richard.*"

"Dad," I interrupt. "She's right. No corn for you. Sorry."

He grunts at me, knowing he lost the argument before it ever began. It was a fool's errand, but something about the smell of butter really makes a person act against his own best interests.

"Thank you, Guy," Mom adds. "We don't need anything. Thanks for asking." She notices the lack of employees in the lobby. "Were you the only one scheduled tonight? No Cate or Kylie?"

"No, not tonight," I lie. "I can handle everything just fine. Plus, Ronnie and Margie are here, right?"

All three of us look over and see Ronnie and Margie sitting on the bottom of the left staircase. They have already cracked open their books for the night. Ronnie is deep into another Lee Child adventure, while Margie has moved on to a biography of Billy Joel. *Who says the elderly cannot fantasize?*

Dad looks unconvinced. "Hmmm," he wonders, "you sure you can handle the lobby tonight? I don't mind helping out. I've seen this movie hundr…"

"No, seriously, I got it. Thank you. You guys just enjoy yourselves."

He probably would have pressed me even more if other customers had not just come through the door behind him.

"He's got it, Richard," Mom affirms. "He's a big boy. We can trust him." She gives me a wink.

They move through the concession line, toward the entry of the main auditorium when I decide to stop them.

"Hey, Mom and Dad?"

They both turn around abruptly to face me, expecting something to be wrong.

"I love you guys."

They smile and look at each other, feeling joint pride as my parents – a sense of *Mission: Accomplished.*

"We love you, Guy."

26

"What's your favorite Billy Joel song?"

I approach Margie and Ronnie on the staircase once it seems as though the drove of people attending tonight's feature has settled in.

"Well, that's a tough question," Margie answers. "I would have to say… hmmm…"

"Oh, come on," Ronnie says, placing his open book down on his knee. "She loves them *all*, Guy. She can't get enough of seventies music, and Billy Joel is occupying our house's airwaves full-time this week, thanks to Alexa."

"Oh, wow, you guys got an Alexa?" I am surprised they would get anything technological placed in their home, especially something as Big-Brother-esque as Alexa, Amazon's music-streaming device. As an avid reader of all of Jack Reacher's adventures, I would have expected Ronnie to veto any such corporate, or maybe even *governmental*, overreach into his home.

"All day long with this Billy Joel," he complains. "We get it – you love playing the piano, drinking beer, falling in love, and eating Italian food. Who doesn't? He thinks he's something special… something unique. This guy should be serenading birthday parties at the Olive Garden, not selling millions of records."

"He's just jealous," Margie whispers to me.

"Jealous? Jealous of what? That *I-talian*?"

"Yes, that '*I-talian*.' He's so talented…"

"Here we go…"

"…the singing, the piano playing, the songwriting…"

"We get it – he can do it all. You should try his agrodolce!"

"He's so *sensual*…" Margie again whispers.

"Now we have it!" Ronnie erupts. "She could take or leave the actual music. She *loves* to imagine that this guy is singin' to her. Am I right?" he zooms in on her reaction.

"Eh," she says with a shrug.

"The only thing I have heard Mr. Joel *truly* sing romantically about is maybe a bottle of red wine. It's all a ruse to impress lonely, impressionable women, like my wife. *To lure them in…*"

"So jealous he is," Margie shakes her head. "You act like you're innocent."

"Me? What have I ever done? You don't hear me carrying on at home, like you do… having Alexa play Doris Day through the night."

"Look what you're reading," Margie points at his book.

"What, *this*?" he says, looking down at it. "Reacher served in the military and bad men chase him unjustifiably everywhere he goes. *Very* bad men. Government schmucks."

"First off, Reacher is not real. Second, he usually meets a new woman in each of those books. Correct?"

"Well, he goes from town to town… He's a vagabond… He meets a lot of new…"

"And what does he do when he gets to know these women?"

"Listen, Reacher is a respectable man! A hero!"

"He has sex with *every single one of them*," Margie says, vindicated.

"Margie!" Ronnie screams, looking around horrified. "Lower your voice with that talk."

"It's true."

"It's *not* true."

"Ronnie, I've read one of them."

Ronnie looks betrayed. "You *what*?"

"It's true."

"Don't you read my Reacher books. You have your shelf at home, and I have mine. These books, they're not for you, Margie… too violent."

"Yeah, yeah," she waves him off. "You see what I'm saying, Guy?" She looks over at me, including me in the conversation once again. "Ronnie's a hypocrite. We all have a type. I like talented men who can sing, write songs, and play an instrument. Ronnie likes women who sleep with vagrants after they witness five minutes of muscle-flexing."

I am thoroughly uncomfortable now. I never want to know about anyone's sexual preferences, but especially not Ronnie's and Margie's.

"Sorry, I didn't mean to start a fight…" I apologize.

Ronnie closes his book. "I can't even read now. You've taken away my joy."

"Welcome to my world," Margie responds.

"What is *that* supposed to mean?" Ronnie asks, deeply offended.

"What even is joy?"

"Oh, well, 'You May Be Right.' I have been waiting to say that for 'The Longest Time,' but 'Don't Ask Me Why' I haven't yet. I just think 'Honesty' is important in a marriage. Right, Margie? It's just a 'Matter of Trust.' At the end of the day, though, I want you 'Just the Way You Are.'" Ronnie holds himself up with pride. "See? Look at me! I should be selling millions of albums right now. Just wait until you hear my song about *junkies* and *masturbation*. Heaven help me…"

"I think it's time you were 'Movin' Out,' Ronnie."

"Oh-ho! You're gonna go there? I'm taking the Alexa with me. The 'Downeaster Alexa'!"

"Oh, I'm going there with you…"

The argument colorfully continues as I walk away. I do not even think they notice I have left. The last thing I hear is something about "Only the Good Die Young," so it is probably good I left when I did.

What am I supposed to do to pass the time tonight? None of my friends are here, Brianna is working, and I cannot watch the movie because I am the only…

Crap! Only now do I realize that Kylie never picked out a loner for me. She left too soon. Not only that, but Caitlyn is not around to talk to a potential either. *This is a disaster*. This whole night is ruined. I cannot work on my "college paper" and I have to listen to "Fred and Ethel" bicker all night.

As I really begin to sink into despair, I hear Ronnie holler from behind. "Hey, where are your little lady friends, Guy?"

"They both have the night off," I say, truly depressed.

"It's just you with us tonight?"

"Yeah, that's right," I say as I slowly walk back toward them. "Why?"

"Listen, why don't you go watch the movie?" Margie offers. "We know that you guys like to go have *fun* while the movies screen…"

"Oh, we do homework, Mrs.…." I begin to say, covering up our massive lie.

"Oh, I know," she says knowingly. "But I'm assuming you don't have any tonight. Correct?"

"That's correct."

"Well, just go ahead and enjoy yourself. You like *Casablanca* don't you?"

"Of course."

"Go ahead then. Ronnie and I can manage."

"Are you sure?" I ask hopefully.

"Guy, we were working this theater, just the two of us, when you were in diapers. We've got it."

"Plus," Ronnie says, "we got some makin' up to do. Don't we, Margie?" Ronnie giggles seductively and it is one of the most horrifying sights I have ever witnessed. It looks as though the Cheshire Cat has swallowed a blue pill, and time is a-tickin'.

"Thank you so much!" I say as I run away. I do not want to witness any more canoodling between these two boomers. It might irrevocably scar me.

The last thing I hear as I throw myself into the auditorium is "You're 'Always a Woman' to me, Margie…"

27

I find a seat, intending to enjoy myself. The idea of finding a loner is on my mind, of course, but that is not my primary goal at the moment. So, I find my usual spot at the back of the theater as the final trailer winds down. A pretty sizable crowd surrounds me tonight – maybe fifty or so – but I do notice that Kylie was correct in her predictions of ageism. The crowd is very grey.

It is also filled with couples, but that does not surprise me either. *Casablanca* is one of, if not *the*, most romantic movies of all time. Pairing it with *La La Land* is a recipe for romance. As I scan the happy couples in front of me, with their heads on their partners' shoulders, I cannot help but wish Brianna were here with me tonight. I really wish I had been nicer to her lately.

You gotta be careful, Guy.

I know I do.

Like The Beatles said, "You're Gonna Lose that Girl."

I cannot even muster a response to my inner demon.

As the movie begins, I sigh in futility. *This shit is hard.*

What is?

All of it.

Oh. Yeah, I know.

Someone in the crowd catches my attention as I try to focus on getting out of my own head. He stands out because, other than me, he appears to be the only other solo person here tonight.

The only loner.

Tonight is the night – the night I act alone. Like a man. I have to take control. After all, if I cannot handle a meager task like talking to a stranger, how am I ever going to manage the task of handling life on my own?

I decide to go to the lobby to get a soda. When I return, I will not return to my usual seat. Instead, I will find a seat near the loner, who appears to be an old man.

At the same time, though, I will not sit anywhere near him. I do not know anything about this loner, but even in the dark, and as briefly as I saw him, I can already tell he is the most intimidating person I have ever encountered. *But this is my task – to be a man.*

I am going to have to muster a lot of strength to talk to this loner tonight. He is not Lauren, and he is certainly not Maya – he is an entirely different animal.

I leave my seat, get my pre-planned soda, and find my new seat. So far, so good. I do not even look over at the loner. I simply sit down to watch *Casablanca*, and I intend to give it my full attention. I am not going to pre-plan my conversation with the man. The only way that I am going to get through to him, I believe, is to strike up a conversation about this movie. I do not think anything else will work.

Just as the title credits onscreen begin to fade away, I see the old man give me a side glance. It is not much, but it is an acknowledgment. While it is dark in the room, obviously, I still cannot help but think I see him scoff as he turns his head back toward the screen.

There is so much greatness in this movie. Aside from the legendary lines.

What strikes you?

First off, Rick is basically an alcoholic. In every scene, he's either pouring a drink or halfway through one already.

Or he's offering one to someone else.

Exactly.

Drunks don't like to drink alone.

They really don't. I wonder why that is?

Makes 'em self-evaluate why they're alone to begin with.

I bet you're right.

I know I am.

How would you know so much about the behavior of drunks anyway?

Intuition?

This love story, though. It really is unique.

How so? I feel like I've seen it a million times.

Well, yeah, because of this movie's influence.

You're probably right.

I know I am.

Please, continue. Moron.

Even though Rick tries to hide his heartbreak from everyone, even by avoiding the song "As Time Goes By," you can't see anything other than heartbreak on his face. He lives with it daily. Nothing can take it away.

Wow, what a great love story. "Hey, kids – guess what? Love will destroy your life!"

It is a great love story for that very reason.
Explain.
Love can alter your life forever. You carry it with you everywhere you go. Love is an emotional tattoo. It makes life worth living. If you never find it, then you never really experience life.
What happens if you lose it, like Rick did?
Silence.
Or maybe like you might?
Silence.
Maybe it's not such a great movie after all, huh?
No, it still is.
How can you say that? It's about everything you're dreading – why you're freaking out right now. Why you're talking to a buncha loners for an imaginary college entry paper. I would think you'd want to avoid this movie at all costs.
Quite the contrary. I feel like I could watch it every day.
Silence.
Oh, now you're silent. For once. I finally broke you.
You mean you finally broke you.
Shut up.
In all honesty, I want you to tell me how could you want to watch Casablanca *every day.*
Because it reminds me that there is a "Paris."
The place where Rick found Ilsa and love?
Exactly.
But he had to leave Paris?
It doesn't matter.

How could it not matter? That's the whole point of the movie! The whole point of love.

It doesn't matter because nothing or no one can ever take away "Paris" from him. It's his forever.

Even if it's gone?

Even if it's gone.

Silence.

It's better to have visited Paris, even for a little while, than never to have gone at all.

The movie and my inner monologue end simultaneously, but a representation of both lingers once the house lights go up. "We'll always have Paris," Rick said.

Damn right we will.

And while I'm lost in my own "la la land," I notice out of the corner of my eye that the old man is staring at me. I am afraid to look over, but I fear I must because if I do not, the stare may go on forever.

I slowly turn my head. When I do, he abruptly stands and exits to the lobby. I cautiously follow. I know he is most likely getting concessions or, even more likely, using the restroom. It is tough for old-timers to make it through one movie without a restroom break, let alone two.

My suspicions are confirmed when I see him close the bathroom door behind him. Just then, my phone rings. I answer the FaceTime.

"How's it going in there?" Kylie asks from my phone screen.

"Pretty good, considering that you left before selecting a loner for me," I say. "Where are you? It sounds really loud."

"Just a party in a field," she says, nonchalantly.

"Of course."

"So, what are you going to do?"

"Don't worry about me… I selected my first loner," I respond proudly.

"Look at you! Growing up… picking out your very own stalking targets…"

"Shut up."

"Let me guess – your loner is a woman in her early twenties with a rockin' bod?" Kylie asks.

I am so happy with myself. "As a matter of fact, Kyle, you're way off. Hold on, I'll send a pic." I send a picture of the old man that I snapped during the middle of the movie.

"Oh, my," Kylie says quietly as she looks at his picture. "Why did you take his photo, you freakin' weirdo? You *are* turning into a stalker."

"I took it because I knew you'd accuse me of finding an attractive woman to talk to, even though I am very happy with Brianna."

"Yeah, good point," she responds. "I would've done that."

"Uh, you already did," I point out.

"Right," she nods onscreen.

"I get that you wanted to prove me wrong, but could you have picked a scarier person, Guy?"

"I needed some variety. I haven't interviewed a man yet."

"And you still haven't," she says. "He looks more beast than man." Suddenly, she looks offscreen and hollers, "Hey, Cate! Come look at Guy's loner!"

"Hey, don't be shoutin' that!" I holler back. "What's Cate doing there anyway? I thought she was going to the movies with her friends?"

"She decided to come with me after I made her feel bad about always being at the theater like some sort of weirdo. Like you!" Kylie laughs.

"Wow, thanks," I mumble. "I wish you guys were here, though. It's easier for me to talk to these loners when you're here to help me."

"Hey, Cate, come hold my phone for a second," she says, handing it off. The angle of the phone readjusts as Caitlyn centers Kylie. "You need to sack up," Kylie says firmly, clapping to every syllable. "Stop being afraid of everything. You and this scary old man aren't a couple of jaguars fighting over the right to lay fifteen lady jaguars."

I have a flashback to the tattooed man sitting next to me in the Mr. Rogers movie. "That's always been a problem for me," I mumble into my phone. *I need to work on my confidence.*

"What?" Kylie asks, irritated. "What is he talkin' about, Cate?"

"Nothing, go on," I encourage.

"Listen, Guy. You're gonna talk to an old dude. You talk to your grandpa, right? Same thing."

"No. Dead."

"What about the other one?"

"I was referring to both. Haven't you seen my parents? If I still had grandparents, they'd be enjoying their golden years aboard the Ark they built."

"They'd be hiding their first-born children and avoiding locusts."

"They'd be taking sides during Passover arguments between my great uncles, Cain and Abel."

"They'd be cheering for the release of Barabbas," I hear Caitlyn shout from off-camera.

"My grandpa would be busy loaning my grandma a rib."

"Nice," both girls say.

"Lots of biblical references, guys," I say. "I'm impressed."

"I wasn't always the mess I am now," Kylie says. Suddenly, from the angle of my phone, I can see her struggling to see something. "There he is," she says, recognizing the loner exiting the restroom. "Time for number two."

"Are you talking about the second feature or the man's bowel movement?"

"Well, he was in there a long time," she replies. I can hear the music start up from inside the auditorium, and she seems to as well. "Sounds like you better get back in there."

"Wish me luck," I say as I walk into *La La Land*.

"Bye, Guy! Good luck!" Caitlyn shouts.

"Try not to have sexual fantasies about this one!"

I end the call before Kylie's entire loud taunt is audible to all.

Luck. I'm gonna need it.

28

I am not sure what it is. Maybe it is this day or this double feature. Maybe it was more impactful that even I had anticipated. Whatever it is, I am completely lost in this movie, and I am all up in my feels. I am not a crier. Crying is acceptable only at funerals and the Grand Canyon, as Ron Swanson would say. Still, despite my inner need to be masculine, I am shedding some hard-earned tears. I have to knock it off, though. If the old man sees me, a loser teenage boy, crying, he is certainly not going to talk to me. In fact, he may exterminate me on the spot to preserve social Darwinism.

I subtly wipe the tears from my eyes as the movie reaches a crescendo. I think masculine thoughts as I try to push out some new chest hairs – the War on Terror, Ernest Hemingway, Ty Cobb ramming his spikes into second basemen, Motorhead, and President Roosevelt delivering a ninety-minute speech after being shot in the chest. *Yeah, that's better.*

After feeling strong enough to choke-slam a bull moose, I get up from my seat to make my way over to the old man, but...

Where is he?!

If I were not so busy worrying about my masculinity, I would have noticed the old man leaving immediately after the movie.

Great. What an idiot I am.

I leave the theater defeated. After being terrified of him all night, I finally felt like I could handle a conversation with him. I only wish I had the chance.

And just like that, I spot him.

At the bar.

The old man is sitting alone at the bar with, seemingly, a shot of whiskey in front of him. Normally, we stop serving drinks an hour before closing down the theater, but I know Margie, and she is kind of a pushover when it comes to pleasing assertive, mean-looking men – in other words, the type of man that Ronnie is not. Everyone has a fantasy, I suppose.

I slowly walk toward the bar, not exactly knowing how to initiate conversation.

"I don't want to be a part of your psychological study, young man," he says with his back toward me.

"I'm sorry?" I muster with what little nerve I have.

He turns his head ninety degrees over his right shoulder. "Us 'loners' do communicate, ya know. As shocking as that may sound."

I am speechless. *They talk? What exactly does he know? He even used the term "loner!"*

"I'm really sorry if I offended you," I stammer. "I can assure you that I have not used the term 'loner' to describe you or any other..."

"Save it," he barks. "I'm not here to listen to you attempt to go through puberty. I just want to sit here with my drink. In silence."

"No problem," I agree. I make my way around the bar. "Would you like anything else?"

"Can't you see that this one is still full?" he says, squinting at me as though he were Clint Eastwood. "What do I look like? A drunk?"

Yes. One hundred percent, yes.

"Absolutely not," I lie. "I'm sorry. I'll leave you alone."

I begin to walk away when he says, "You don't strike me as the type to enjoy a romance from the forties."

"Oh, *Casablanca*?" I ask, turning back around. "Yeah, I love it." I pause before deciding if I should really say my next thought out loud. I go for it. "You don't strike me as someone who enjoys musicals."

He growls at me, but in a playful sort of way. Like a bear does with its food before devouring it. "I'm a filmmaker. I love all sorts of movies."

"You're a filmmaker?" I say, shaking my head. "And you're hanging around *here*? In small-town Missouri?"

"Even better – I'm from here."

"I'm surprised I haven't heard of you," I think aloud. "I'm such a movie buff."

"Well, I could be wrong, but it seems as though you have your head firmly planted inside your asshole."

Fair enough.

"Have you made anything recently?"

"Not recently, no. That's probably the real reason you haven't heard of me."

"What was your biggest movie, if I may ask?"

He thinks for a moment. "Probably *Killer Be Killed*."

"No shit?!"

"No shit."

The realization finally comes to me. "You're Jim Morris!"

"That's right."

"I can't believe…"

"I'm out in public?" he promptly cuts me off.

I try to sidestep the subject of his notoriously reclusive lifestyle. I, of course, knew what the younger, 1970s version of Jim Morris looked like, but no one had photographed him in years. If I remember correctly, the Academy Awards may have even prematurely included him in one of their "In Memoriam" segments back in the late 1980s. "That movie… It's one of the greatest documentaries ever made."

"Thank you." His response sounds like something between a groan and a burp.

"So, what are you doing here? In this small, rinky-dink theater?"

He looks down. "I'm having a drink."

I look at his drink as well. "It doesn't seem as though you're making much headway. Seriously, you can have whatever you want, on the house."

"No thanks, this will do," he says, firmly holding the glass.

"I can't help but keep thinking that you should be living somewhere else," I say bemused.

"Like where?"

"I don't know… like New York or L.A. or somewhere… bigger. More important."

"New York and L.A. aren't home. Harlan is."

"Are you retired then?" I ask.

"You could say that," he mumbles incoherently.

"How's retirement treating you?"

"Much like the rest of my life. Shit."

I feel myself making big eyes. "Oh, I'm sorry."

"Whatever."

"It can't be all bad. You get to go to movies whenever you want and drink afterwards."

He looks up at me, disgusted. "I don't drink."

"What?" I ask truly confused.

"This," he says, holding up the glass so that he can look at me through it, "is not for drinking. It's for remembering."

I find the barstool behind me and, without looking, pull it under myself with my right leg. I am locked in. "What do you mean?"

"I always order a drink when I'm out, especially after watching a movie," he says. "I like to just... look at it. Stare at it. But I never drink it. I'm a recovering alcoholic."

"How long have you been sober?" I ask timidly. "If you don't mind me asking."

"Six months, give or take a week or so," he says.

I clear my throat as a way of organizing my next question.

"What?" he asks. "Just say it."

"I just don't understand why you order drinks if you're recovering. It seems like such a temptation or... punishment."

"It is," he agrees. "I do it because it reminds me of my present and of my past. My younger years were fueled by this stuff. Whiskey in particular. It's a bad mother."

"So I've heard."

"You're not a drinker?"

"I'm still in high school."

"That's not what I asked."

"No, I'm not a drinker. Never appealed to me."

"That's good," he says. "But that doesn't mean that something else won't get you. Something always gets everybody." He swirls the liquid inside the glass. "I like this stuff, though. Even now. I like the pain of its presence. The sight, the smell... it smells like failure."

"Failure?"

"I've had plenty of it in my life."

"How so?" I ask. "I mean, you made one of the most influential documentaries of all time. I don't know what else you've done, but that movie alone..."

"You don't get it, kid," he says firmly. "That's not what life is about."

"Life isn't about *massively succeeding* in your profession?"

"No."

"What's it about then?"

"It has a different face for each person," he says softly. "Mine had soft skin, green eyes, and a laugh that could warm any cynic."

"I think I know what you mean," I say just as softly.

"Oh, really?" he laughs the laugh of a still-smoking chimney. "Puberty boy has a girlfriend, eh?"

"I do," I reply terrified but amused.

"What's her name?" he asks.

"Brianna," I answer. "What's her name?" I ask in turn.

"Her name was Annie," he says with faraway eyes – the eyes of a veteran recalling the origins of an ancient battlefield scar.

I cannot help but notice the use of the word "was" in his reply, though. "What happened?"

"What did I tell you?" he snarls. "Didn't I already tell you that I don't want to be a part of your hippy-dippy experiment?" He pushes his drink away. I can tell he wants to leave, and I can also tell that there is nothing that can stop this man from doing what he wants to do.

"No, please, I'm sorry. I didn't mean to pry. I just... I'm just trying to learn."

"Learn about what?" he spits.

"What to expect," I answer. "After all of this. I'm not sure how to handle what comes next."

"Get in line," he says harshly. "None of us do."

"But you have wisdom, guidance..."

"The only wisdom I have is in the area of what *not* to do."

"Then that's what I need to know."

The old man's eyes peer up from the bar and look through my soul. "I don't want to be referenced or quoted in any paper, college-bound or otherwise."

"Deal," I say certainly.

"It's simple, kid. All you need to know about life was already presented to you tonight."

"What do you mean?"

"The key to understanding life is Paris."

29

"The key to life is the plot device in *Casablanca*?" I ask, truly confused.

"And *La La Land*," Mr. Morris affirms.

"I want to believe you," I say, "I just don't quite understand."

"Let's do some film theory together," he says. "Okay, kid?"

"I'm ready," I reply.

"What is the lesson of *Casablanca*?"

I remember my inner monologue from earlier. "It's about embracing love when you have the chance, but that doesn't mean a person's life has to end when the love does. You can always go back to it... remember it. Like Rick did with Paris. The important thing wasn't that he continued that old strain of love. He had it once. That's what was important."

"You're a regular Roger Ebert, aren't you?" the old man chuckles. It is a sound that seems alien to his very essence. "How did you learn so much about storytelling and film?"

"My parents own this theater."

"You're Richard and Carol's kid?"

"That's me."

"I remember when you used to run up and down these aisles like a maniac when you were barely old enough to make full sentences. You know, you could really kill a movie's enjoyment back then."

"And now I basically run this place." I am not bragging when I say it. In fact, the words are melancholy.

"The parents are getting' up there, aren't they?" he asks, his voice sad. "They're about as old as me."

"They are," I agree. "So I take on a lot of the responsibility of this place. I'm the one who sets up these double-features."

"Look at you," he nods almost proudly. "You paired these two films tonight?"

"I did."

"I guess you do know what you're doing."

"I do it on instinct. I don't overthink it. Before tonight, I never even thought about the Paris-connection between these two movies."

"It's all over the place, isn't it?" he smiles.

"It really is," I chuckle. "In *La La Land*, the Eiffel Tower represents Sebastian and Mia's relationship. It's like the pinnacle moment for when they're each succeeding, both financially and artistically in their careers. And in their love."

"Why do you think that is?" the old man asks, leading.

"*Casablanca*?" I suggest.

"I don't know what Damien Chazelle intended, but yeah, that's all I can think about when I rewatch this movie. The ending implies that. The whole movie is driving toward the idea that love – the true, fiery, passionate, kind – cannot be sustained. But then we get that moment – where we see that it's possible. Love can succeed if we try hard enough, in the 'city of stars,' if you will. But..."

"But then it doesn't," I conclude.

"We crash back into reality, into the world that exists outside of 'la la land,' where that kind of love is usually unattainable. It *can* happen, but only for a brief moment."

"Like Paris in *Casablanca*."

"Exactly."

"It's really kind of sad," I say.

"Life *is* really kind of sad," he agrees. "Look at Emma Stone's character. She says she was driven to succeed by her aunt who lived in Paris. She was a fool who dared to dream to be an artist. What was her reward? 'She lived in her liquor and died with a flicker.'"

The old man brings the glass back toward him. The melody of sharing this moment with the legendary Jim Morris almost makes me cry again, but I then remember President Roosevelt. This man, though... he has *lived* a life. A crazy life full of success. Yet, it is a life I do not want to know.

Or do I?

"You forgot the line that comes next in the song," I remind him.

"What?" he says, snapping back into reality.

"It goes, 'She lived in her liquor, died with a flicker, but I'll always remember the flame.'"

"'The flame,'" he remembers with a smile. "That's a good line."

I nod. "You had a flame. That movie you made. Annie..."

The old man snaps his head toward me. The very sound of her name seems to sober this recovering addict like a simultaneous cold shower and hot cup of coffee. After seeing my reaction, and anticipating my urgent apology for uttering his beloved's name, he eases back down. "Yeah, Annie."

"What happened to her?" I ask against all better judgment.

His lip curls at the very thought of opening up to me, a snot-nosed little punk who can quote musicals better than he can. "We got married," he finally releases. "Had two kids."

"Your Paris became a reality," I say with renewed excitement.

"And just like the Nazis in World War II, I burned it down."

"Oh," I say with renewed embarrassment.

"I ruined it, kid," he mumbles, gripping his drink harder than ever. "It's gone."

"How?" I ask softly.

"I drank away the best years of our life." He lets loose the words like a belch after a big meal. "I thought succeeding in my career as a filmmaker would make me happy. I always wanted to be a director, and I chased after it like a madman. And after *Killer Be Killed* became a hit, I grabbed onto the whirlwind of the moment and never let go. Until it was too late."

"She stayed with you through it all?"

"She did. But I took her for granted. I was constantly away, on film shoots or at meetings or networking with new people or letting off steam in bars. My life was completely about movies." He shakes his head at the memory. "We had two kids, Emma and Stephen. But I was hardly there for them. Annie raised them. As the years went by, I lost track of my family. When I did finally make an appearance at home, I barely recognized them. Emma would have new braces, Stephen would be a foot taller, and Annie would have a new haircut. Even stranger, Annie would look *older*. Every time I saw her, I saw the years slide away from us. I saw time missing moments – the time that could have been spent at home. Lazy Sundays where our family watched TV, played in the yard, or had a barbeque together. But those things never happened."

"Why didn't they?" I ask.

"Aren't you listening?" the old man sighs. "I pissed it all away. I chose my career over my family." He pauses to catch his breath. I can tell that he is not in great health, even for his age. He has lived a rugged life. "I chose my addictions over them, too. My drinking spiraled at home. When I was around them, I wanted to escape. I felt like I was wasting time at home... I was wasting valuable time that could have been put toward writing a new film or discovering a new subject to document. More than anything, I wanted to preserve my name in the industry that I loved most – film. I *needed* to be an important filmmaker. My life was pointless otherwise."

"When did you realize that wasn't what you wanted anymore?"

The old man is lost in his memories. His eyes are faraway. "When she cheated on me. That's when I knew. We always had 'Paris,' but I was the one who left it first. I don't even blame her. She knew I didn't want to be at home, to be a family man. What was she supposed to do? She needed to feel love again, like the kind we shared all those years ago. By the time I got my act together, though, it was too late. The damage had already been done. I spent the rest of our time together drinking away my sorrows of lost years and love. I was substituting booze for happiness."

"I'm really sorry..."

"She died," he says, disregarding my attempt to console.

"When?"

He looks down at his drink. "About six months, give or take a week or so."

And now it all makes sense.

"We all yearn for it to end, kid," he says looking over at me fully for the first time. "We want school to end, the job to end, the toddler years to end, the fights to end, the nights to end, the career to end, the marriage to end, our problems to end, our lives... all of it. We can't wait for it all to end. But when we're finally faced with the end, we don't know how to deal with it. Fear and uncertainty creep in. Suddenly, we feel infantile in our abilities to fight against it, and we are. It's pointless. The end comes, and it's never what we want when we finally get it. That's the lesson, kid."

"I thought the lesson was 'Paris.'"

"It's all the same thing," he clarifies. "Life is about grabbing onto the moments, the love, that will define us and make it all worthwhile. The problem is that we usually don't recognize those moments until it's too late, when we're at the end. Do you really think Rick appreciated his relationship with Ilsa while they were in Paris? Absolutely not. He was just loving getting hammered and laid. Before arriving at Casablanca, he didn't think he'd spend the rest of his life reliving those moments. We never do."

The old man stands up from the bar, pushing his whiskey toward me.

"Thanks for talking to me, Mr..."

"Jim," he answers. "Just Jim."

"Jim," I comply. "Thank you."

The old man begins to make his way from the bar, but he is slow. His body clearly hurts. Despite his much-desired need to go home as quickly as possible, he stops and leans against the bar next to me. "Earlier, you said you couldn't believe I was still living here, over in Harlan, of all places. I used to think like that, too. I wanted to live anywhere else. That's probably why I wanted to get away and travel as much as I did. It was exciting at first, but then I really started to look around, outside of the big cities. I watched endless small towns in America fly by the windows of my car or planes, and once I got older, I always thought the same thing. My life wouldn't work anywhere else. I don't mean anything to those people – not really. Not like I did to the people of Harlan. Those towns didn't feel like home to me, because they weren't. My home was where I met and fell in love with Annie. It was where we bought our first house together, where we had our kids. I didn't care that our town didn't have a lot to offer in terms of opportunity or entertainment. It had offered me something more – a place to enjoy my family. I could look in any direction and find a memory that meant something to me. When you're young, you overlook things like that. Of course, I didn't realize that until it was too late."

While I cannot verbalize a response, I know he is right. There is nothing I can say that can match the sentiment he just offered. He conveys wisdom that can only be obtained with age and experience, and he has clearly had his fair share of both.

"Thanks for the drink," he says, throwing on his jacket.

"Of all of the gin joints, in all the towns, in all the world, you walked into mine."

Jim stops mid-step and turns his head ninety degrees again. "Don't push it, kid."

As he leaves, I suppress a laugh and begin to wipe down the bar for the night. And then the old man says the unexpected.

"I think this is the beginning of a beautiful friendship."

PART FIVE

TOUCH OF EVIL

GOODFELLAS

30

"Did you hear about Kylie?!"

Brianna and I barely get through the door before Caitlyn delivers the news.

"Her mom found out that she went to that party, like two weeks after it happened, and just now grounded her."

"You mean that party that she took you to?" I ask.

"Yeah, that one," Caitlyn continues. "I left somewhat early, like around midnight. Since I didn't drink, I got to drive myself home when I wanted. I guess Kylie got hammered, though. You saw her story on Snapchat, I'm assuming. Anyway, she was riding home with Anthony and they got stopped by the cops on the way home."

"Are you serious?" Brianna asks. "How did I not hear about this?"

"She was trying to lay low," Caitlyn says.

"That's kind of surprising given her need to constantly achieve clout," I add.

"Very true, but she had to keep low so that her parents didn't find out that she was taken to the police station."

"They took her in?" Brianna is fully enthralled in this story. "How did she get home without calling a parent?"

"She called her aunt and had her lie and say she was her mom," Caitlyn continues. "I guess the aunt knows the drill by now. This isn't Kylie's first run-in with the law. But anyway, I think the aunt slipped up a few days ago and, well… now Kylie's done for."

"How bad is it?" I ask.

"If Kylie is not scheduled to work, then she is on total lock-down. No friends, no laptop, no phone."

"Holy shit," Brianna and I say in unison.

"Exactly," Caitlyn nods. "She's gonna die from withdrawals."

"Her thousands of followers are going to think she's dead if she doesn't post something by nine in the morning," I say. "So you didn't get in any trouble?"

"I didn't do anything to *get* into trouble," Caitlyn responds.

"Look at you," I laugh. "You were right."

"I don't want to toot my own horn, but yeah. I told her this was gonna happen."

"I guess we won't be seeing her tonight," Brianna says. "She's not scheduled, is she?"

"No," I answer. "But hey, we have enough to play a game of handball if you want. Are you gonna hang out for a while, B?"

"I have to be at home by eight o'clock for my Netflix party," she answers, "but yeah, until then, I'll hang."

"Netflix party?" Caitlyn asks.

"It's my homework for College English," she answers.

Caitlyn is in a different college English course than Brianna, and I am not currently enrolled in college classes, so the two of us are rightly confused. "How is that homework?" I ask.

"Our class voted on a film to watch, so we watch it together, from home, and discuss it while it plays. After it's over, we all have to write an essay about it," Brianna explains.

"You're doomed, Guy," Caitlyn says.

"Why is that?" I ask.

"Look at how people watch movies now," she says simply. Caitlyn is completely right. In our era, the idea of having to drive somewhere to enjoy a movie with a communion of people is obsolete. Now, you can enjoy whatever movie you want from home, *and* with the people you want – not just a smattering of strangers who might ruin the movie for you anyway. The Bristol is doomed.

I am doomed.

"Eight o'clock?" I reaffirm.

"That's right," she says.

I am always upset when Brianna has to leave me, but her timing will actually be perfect tonight. I need to conduct a loner interview, and I cannot exactly do that if she is still here at the theater.

Given this information and tonight's schedule, I approach Ronnie and Margie as they occupy their usual spots on the stairs. "Hey…"

"Good lineup tonight, Guy," Ronnie compliments. "You're getting better and better at selectin' the old ones."

"Thanks, Ron," I say.

"Got some homework to do?" Margie asks.

"Yeah. Is it okay…?"

"Go ahead," she giggles. "You kids."

Ronnie looks up at me with a devilish grin. "You hold onto that one, son."

"Oh, Brianna?" I ask, pointing with my thumb.

"Yeah. She's a keeper, Guy. So sweet. And what a looker... Oy vey, I bet she's a handful!" Ronnie fans himself down with his novel.

"Ronnie!" Margie hushes him as I laugh in agreement. "They're still high schoolers!"

"Hey, you and me were still kids when I used to pick you up in my car after football games," Ronnie says, leaning in and nudging her shoulder. Margie pushes him away, equal parts angry and humored. He then turns his attention back to me and says, "You just do what I told you, Guy. I know a good lady when I see one." He pulls Margie in close.

"Yeah, I think I'll hold onto her."

31

"Are you looking forward to college?" Brianna asks Caitlyn as she volleys the handball over to her side of the court. I am working as line judge and score keeper during their game.

"Yeah, I think so," Caitlyn says, hitting the ball back. She scores the point.

"Three-to-two, Cate," I say, handing the ball back to Caitlyn. This game is decidedly less aggressive than the ones I participate in. Instead, it is more meditative, which is actually nice.

"I mean, I'm nervous to live with a roommate in a dorm and everything," Caitlyn continues, "but I'll get used to it. Probably similar to basketball camp."

"Just hope you don't get stuck with someone who parties all the time or wants to bring dudes back late at night," Brianna says.

"Three-to-three."

"What about you?" Caitlyn asks. "How are you feeling?"

Yes, I too would like to hear this answer.

"I wouldn't really say I'm *nervous* actually. In fact, I'm kind of excited."

"Four-to-three, Bri."

Excited? How can she be excited?

"Why are you excited?" Caitlyn asks.

Yes, why? Thank you, Caitlyn.

"Well, because I do like learning and taking different types of classes," Brianna says.

"Just don't take Literature 101," I pipe in, remembering Maya's adventure.

Brianna stops and looks at me. "What?"

"Nothing, sorry," I respond. "Five-to-three."

"What about all of the new people?" Caitlyn asks. "Your roommate, suitemates, people on your floor in your dorm... You worried that it'll be hard to meet all those new people and actually get along with them?"

"I think about it a lot, but I think I'll be okay."

"Six-to-three."

Brianna serves the ball and a couple of volleys pass back and forth before they speak again. "I'm gonna miss doing this with you guys," Brianna says. "I always had fun visiting Guy at work... seeing you and Kylie."

"Six-to-four."

"I know," Caitlyn agrees. "These nights on the roof were some of the best of my life."

"Six-to-five."

"Does it overwhelm you?" Brianna asks her. "You know, starting over, but also starting something completely new at the same time?"

"Six-to-six."

"Yeah, it does. I try not to dwell on it."

"How can you not do that, though?"

"I dunno... I always just try to focus on accomplishing the next thing. High school diploma, college diploma, job, marriage, house, kids..."

"Death," I add.

"What?" Caitlyn asks.

"Nothing," I respond. "Seven-to-six."

"There's always something else we have to accomplish," Caitlyn continues. "We always have one more step we need to ascend. That keeps my mind busy. Keeps it off the scary things."

"Scary things like what?" Brianna says.

"Eight-to-six, Caitlyn."

"Like all of the uncertainty. And like you said, meeting all of these new people. It's scary and exciting at the same time. We might potentially meet some people who completely change our lives. But that's the thing – it could be for the better or for…"

"Worse," I complete. "Nine-to-six."

"Right," Caitlyn says, serving again. "That really freaks me out. But if we don't try new things, then, ya know…" Suddenly she stops talking, and the three of us all know why.

You'll end up like Guy.

"Nine-to-seven."

"I know what you mean," Brianna agrees. "It freaks me out, too. We have to make so many decisions in such a short time that will change our lives forever. We set in motion things that we can never really change… without starting all over again. No one wants that."

"Nine-to-eight."

"Do you know what you're majoring in yet?" Brianna asks.

"Sports therapy. What about you?"

"I'm not sure yet. I think I want to just experience college as a freshman and not make any huge decisions yet. Just see how I feel after that first year."

"Tied game."

"You'll figure it out," Caitlyn says.

"Yeah, I know. I just want to make sure I take my time and really think over everything. I feel like I don't always make the best decisions for myself in the moment. I don't give myself enough time."

"Ten-to-nine. Game point, Brianna."

"Sometimes you have to have to examine everything on your own, without any input from anyone else," Caitlyn advises. "Because other people can try and guide you too much to make a decision that would be best for them, but not *you*."

"I think you are one hundred percent correct."

"Game. Brianna wins."

I grab the handball and put it in the bucket that holds it between sessions.

"You gonna play winner, Guy?" Caitlyn asks me.

"No, I think I'm good," I respond. Their game of handball may have been meditative for the two of them, but it was anything but that for me.

"We should hang out more," Brianna suggests to Caitlyn, smiling.

Yes, you're just two of a kind, aren't you? Two burgeoning young adults who need to get away. Away from this town… this theater… me.

"We should," Caitlyn agrees. "Too bad our universities are so far apart."

"Well, we'll just have to get together on the weekends. Meetup at the theater here when I visit Guy." Brianna comes in and hugs me from the side. It is conversely the most pleasant and painful hug I have ever received from her. She kisses me on the cheek and then pulls out her phone. "Seven thirty. I should probably get back."

"Time to party!" Caitlyn says.

"Exactly," Brianna laughs. "This is my type of college party, for sure." She wraps me in another hug and says, "Text me after you close down tonight, okay?"

"Yep, I will," I agree. I hug her back deeply. While I do not intend to make Brianna think anything is wrong with me, I feel as though she senses it. She looks me in the eyes, squinting, briefly, to evaluate my emotional state. "I love you," I tell her.

"Love you, Guy."

With that, Brianna leaves for her first of many college adventures.

32

"Do you know who's here tonight?" Margie rushes over and asks Caitlyn and me as we descend the staircase.

"No. Who?"

What unusual person would ever visit our tiny, hometown theater in Hudson, Missouri?

"Wade Parker," Margie says.

"Oh, she's swooning again!" Ronnie shouts. "He's too young for ya, Margie!"

"Seriously?" Caitlyn asks. "That's crazy!"

"He's here for the double feature!" Margie confirms. "Been here since the start."

I can see that this news hits Caitlyn particularly hard. She blames me for missing out on interacting with someone actually important.

"He came for *Touch of Evil*?" I ask. "Great taste."

I like this guy already.

"Was he with anyone?" Caitlyn quickly asks. It is the inevitable question for anyone who has read his most-recent book.

"He was by himself," Margie says.

Once again, Kylie is not here to pick out my loner tonight, but that is actually okay. I do not need her assistance tonight. I already have one selected.

Unlike every loner before, I do not need Kylie or Caitlyn to point out tonight's target. I know Wade Parker. Well, I do not know him *personally*, but everyone around here knows who he is. He is one of the area's only semi-celebrities, alongside the previously-thought-dead Jim Morris. He is a published author whose first book, *Harlan Sacrifice*, was a big hit nationwide. Since then, his popularity dipped rapidly. Everyone around here started doubting his ability immediately. It was pathetic. It was like they were wanting him to fail... *just waiting for it.*

Parker got the last laugh, though. His newest book, *Petrarchan Girl*, was another smash, even bigger than his first. He won over a whole new fanbase with it – particularly women of all ages. Everyone wondered who the "mystery girl" he wrote about was, but he never spoke about her or their romance in detail. "The truth is a lot less salacious than it seems," he would say on occasion.

Since then, Parker has kept pretty quiet. Word is that the success of *Petrarchan Girl* created renewed interest in his intellectual properties, though. Late last year, a film adaptation of *Harlan Sacrifice* was announced, although it is currently under the working title *The Old Must Die*, a reference to the last line – and overall theme – of his inaugural book. I guess Hollywood thought that the mentioning of our small town of Harlan in the title was a bit too inside for mainstream audiences. Parker, however, has not commented on the potential film, nor has he announced his follow-up book to *Petrarchan Girl*. It has been two years since that novel was published. That is the longest break he has ever taken between books, but I guess he has earned it. I can only assume that he is awaiting another moment of inspiration to strike him before he begins his next literary journey.

I hesitate talking to him, though. I do not find him intimidating per se, certainly not in the way Jim Morris was, but I cannot imagine that Wade Parker would want to talk to me. I am an eighteen-year-old high schooler and he is a thirty-year-old accomplished author.

Regardless, I will try.

Since Kylie is not scheduled tonight, and since Brianna just left, Caitlyn and I do not play a game on the roof. We never do with just the two of us. There is something about having a third person around that immediately changes the dynamic – livens it up. So, I decide to watch *Goodfellas*. Ronnie and Margie have proven that they can handle the concession stand without me, so why not?

I could use the quiet of the movie, even one as loud at times as *Goodfellas*, to prepare for the end of my night. I am feeling a bit more nervous than usual. I need the extra time to prepare myself. I need to appear confident when speaking to Parker. *I need to know my stuff.*

Plus, I really want to watch this movie again. I cannot help it. Martin Scorsese is like a drug for me. I cannot get enough of his movies. I shoot each one of them up, directly into a bulging vein, the moment I get a chance to watch one. Like tonight.

"Come on, watch it with me," I beg Caitlyn. "You can star-gaze Wade Parker at the same time…"

"There's no one to run the counter if I do, Guy," Caitlyn says, not knowing just how competent Ronnie and Margie still are.

"Those two can handle it," I answer. "And we'll watch the door and go help if we feel like there's a rush."

"Plus, I still kind of need you tonight," I say.

Caitlyn is confused. "What do you mean?"

"I mean, I'm still interviewing loners…"

"Yeah? And?"

I nod my head over toward the auditorium door.

"You want me to go talk to *him*?" she asks me in astonishment.

"What's the big deal?" I say. "Plus, you wanted to talk to him anyway."

"I don't know…"

"Caitlyn."

"What?"

"Please," I plead. "I need your help."

She huffs nervously. "Fine. I'll go talk to him for you. But that's it."

"Come on. Don't be that way."

"This isn't really my type of movie," she hems and haws.

"Have you seen it before?"

"No. I don't like gangster movies. Too violent. And corny."

"I assure you it's not."

"Violent or corny?"

"Corny. It's super violent."

"No, Guy."

I grab her hand. "Please, come on. I promise you'll like it."

She frowns. "Fine."

And she does.

33

Goodfellas reaches its climax during the final montage, and I can tell Caitlyn is enjoying it, perhaps even more than her brief conversation with Parker earlier. When the movie is over, I lean over to her. "Well?" I ask simply.

"It was amazing," she admits.

"I told you!"

"You did. But I have to go to the counter now. I need to clean up so that you can have your little therapy session."

Oh, yeah. With the excitement of Scorsese, I kind of forgot about tonight's mission.

"You better get over there," she says, pointing to Parker sitting in his seat. He is off in the corner, totally alone. "Take good notes tonight!"

I approach him. He quickly looks over and says, "You Guy?"

"That's me," I answer.

"Your girlfriend told me about a writing project you're working on. Is that right?"

"Yes. Well, except the part about her being my girlfriend."

He looks me over, skeptical.

"What is it you need to know, Guy?"

Who was Anna? Was she real? Was that her real name? Have you talked to her since?

"Let me guess," he answers himself. "'Who was Anna?' Am I right?"

"No, that's not what this paper is about."

Parker looks relived. "Oh, okay. I just figured this was... never mind. Do you want to be a writer or something?"

"No, not really," I answer.

"What do you want to be then?"

It sounds funny, but no one has really asked me that question since I was in grade school and offered such absurd answers as "astronaut" or "Sasquatch hunter." Everyone knew I was taking over this theater, so why bother indulging my imagination? I already had a firm reality.

"I don't really know," I say honestly. "I mean, my dream scenario would probably be a movie director. I've been working at this theater for as long as I can remember. I don't think I'd know how to do anything else."

Parker chuckles. "I know what you mean. I was a huge movie buff growing up, too. In fact, I also wanted to be a director for a moment. But then the opportunity arose for me to write."

"What opportunity was that?"

"Are you familiar with my work?"

"Yeah, I know them all, Mr. Parker."

"Ew. Don't do that."

I am confused. "Do what?"

"Don't call me Mr. Parker. Just Wade, please."

"Okay, Wade. Yes, I know your work well."

"Well, then you know the answer. My first book was about the hardships my friend faced. I felt as though I needed to tell his story so that people could know more about, and understand, people like him better. I could only do that through writing."

"It was a great book."

He squints an eye. "I shouldn't ask this."

"Go ahead," I press. "Please."

"An author always wants to know which of his books works the best for each of his readers. It's indulgent and self-serving."

"You want to know which of your books I liked the best?"

Wade shrugs his shoulders. "Yeah, I kinda do."

"Well, *Petrarchan Girl* is great."

He smiles. "I knew it. That seems to be everyone's favorite."

"But," I continue, "I *really* loved your book about devil worshippers."

"*Return of the Devil*?!" he laughs.

"Yeah!" I join him. "It was so good."

"I can't believe you liked that one. No one ever picks it."

"It's probably just because they haven't read it."

"Based on the sales, you're probably right in that assumption," he smiles. "Thanks for that. I'm going to mentally list that as one of the best compliments I've ever gotten."

"What *is* the best compliment you've ever gotten?" Wade immediately begins to infectiously laugh, and I quickly join him. "What? It must be good."

"Oh, it was."

"Was it about *Petrarchan Girl*?"

"It was."

"Tell me," I ask eagerly.

"I was at a book signing in southern Missouri," Wade tells me with an enormous smile. "I don't know what it is about my Missouri audience, but they take much more ownership over me – they are bolder when they talk to me. Anyway, I was signing books for a long line of, mostly, women. They were of all ages, but then the eldest of the group approached me. She was probably seventy years old. When I asked her who I should make the book out to, she blew off my question and asked her own. 'Are you still with Anna?' she asked. I chuckled and gave my usual response, 'The truth is really not that exciting.' The old woman, whose name was Dorothy, then told me something I'll never forget. She leaned down, looked *deeply* into my eyes, firmly held out her copy of *Petrarchan* Girl, and said, 'Son, if you had written this book about me, and if I were thirty years younger or you were thirty years older, winter would turn to summer before you ever saw the outdoors again.' It was probably the greatest line I had ever heard, but she did not laugh. She was completely serious."

"How could you possibly respond to something like that?" I ask.

Wade shrugs. "I told her the truth. I said, 'What a shame for the both of us.'"

We begin to laugh together again, and then I say, "You must have the best untold stories."

He takes a moment to evaluate my face. "So you really know my stuff, huh?"

"I'm a huge fan," I admit.

"And you *don't* want to know about Anna at all?"

"Well," I look to the side, "I mean, sure I do. But that's not what this is about. I promise."

Wade rubs his chin in thought. "I'll help you out, and then you can ask me one question about *Petrarchan Girl*, if you want."

"That'd be amazing," I agree.

"But," he quickly adds, "if I'm going to be honest with you, then you need to be honest with me when I have questions. Deal?"

"Deal."

34

"Why are you back in the area?" I ask Wade. "Shouldn't you be on a book tour or something?"

Wade laughs. "My last book did well, but not long enough to sustain a two-year tour."

"Are you writing another book now?"

Wade squirms a bit. "I am, but it's taking a minute."

"Why is this one taking so long?"

An awkward pause.

"In the past, for me to write, I needed to feel as uncomfortable as possible. With the first book, that was easy. The topic of suicide is obviously uncomfortable. As you can imagine, it really messes with your psyche when you're inside the mind of a first-person narrator like that for months. That's why I stepped away from being 'uncomfortable' with my next two books. I tried to write and enjoy myself. That, however, was clearly a mistake. Audiences obviously didn't want me to enjoy myself, because they didn't enjoy my 'happy' output. And then Anna happened..." Wade trails off. "*Petrarchan Girl* was incredibly easy to write, but difficult at the same time."

"How so?"

"Well, I had a dying urge to write it."

"What was the urge?"

"It's exactly what I said in the book. I needed the world to know that it was possible for someone as beautiful as Anna to exist. Her beauty, inside and out, drove me to write that book. I was a man possessed. No one could have stopped me from getting out that story. I would have written it down on rolls of toilet paper if necessary."

"Well, it sounds like it was completely easy to write it then. Why then did you say you were uncomfortable?"

"What could be more uncomfortable than writing a romance? That was completely out of my wheelhouse. Before Anna, I wrote about violent people and intense situations. *Petrarchan Girl* was the opposite of that. The only intensity in that story was that of my passion for her."

"She kind of brought out the best in you."

"That's what people tell me. And that's why I'm hounded everywhere I go about who she is. No one ever believes my answers anyway."

"Why not?"

"Because they believe what they want to believe. If I told them the truth, they'd be unhappy with it. If I told them a salacious lie, they'd be unhappy with it. I guess that's what art is all about, though. Interpretation."

"I don't know who 'Anna' is, but when I was reading your book, I felt as though you were writing about my girlfriend."

"Maybe I was. What's her name?" he laughs. "Kidding, obviously."

"I'm sure she wishes," I join in.

"What's your girlfriend like?" Wade asks.

I find myself in a difficult situation. How do I describe Brianna to the man who so eloquently wrote about Anna, his love. My words would never do Brianna justice to him.

"Her name is Brianna," I begin. "And she is... I don't even know."

"Go ahead, man," Wade urges me. "Try."

I take a breath. "She's like an orb of energy."

Wade's brow furrows. "Orb of energy?"

I shake my head, "Sorry, I think I was trying to sound like you or something. Like an author."

Wade laughs. "Don't try to sound like me. That's the first rule. If you are going to succeed in anything, whether it's in a job or with a girl, you need to be honest. Definitely do not try to sound like an author. They spend too much time trying to be flowery and impress their readers with how effectively they can use a thesaurus. The best authors speak honestly and directly. Plain and simple. That's how you move someone. So try again, but this time, I want you to speak honestly about how you feel about Brianna."

"She's everything to me."

"Good. Go on."

"When I see her, she immediately makes my day better. When she's not there, I want to give up and go home. She's like a human adrenaline shot. Her personality is as radiant as her outside beauty. I never laugh so hard as when she's around, and I never hurt so bad as when she's absent."

"What do you love most about her?"

"How she never gives up on me. I get down on myself a lot with stress about the future… my parents, my job, my life in general… but she always calms me down. I feel so relaxed around her. I would follow her anywhere."

"That's a lot better, Guy," Wade says, patting me on the shoulder. "Don't you think?"

"Yeah," I agree. "If I only had the nerve to tell her that stuff in person."

"Never be afraid to tell someone how she makes you feel."

"You must be a killer with the ladies," I laugh.

Wade shakes his head. "Lady."

"You mean...?" I start to ask. I am surprised I did not know this piece of information about a local "celebrity," but Wade Parker is notoriously private. Like Stanley Kubrick post-*Barry Lyndon* reclusive.

"Yep," Wade answers succinctly. He does not have to say any more than that. Anyone who has read his book knows exactly what that means.

"Isn't it hard, though?" I ask against all better instincts.

"To be in a relationship with someone other than 'Anna'?" he asks. "Of course it is."

"Why do you do it then?"

Wade sighs. "Because it's more difficult to be alone. I can distract myself with someone else, with all of the maintenance that goes into a normal relationship. I can even pretend that I *am* with Anna at times. But if I'm alone... That's not a good place for me. It's easy to slip into despair and, frankly, give up."

"Why would that make you want to give up?"

"Because Anna is somewhere out there still – maybe even somewhere relatively close, which means that a 'happy life' for me is also relatively close. That's a tough concept to wrap your head around."

"Do you think she'd want you to be with someone else?" I ask boldly.

Wade chuckles in incredulity. "That's a question I can't honestly answer. I can only assume, though, that she *is* with someone else, whether it is that old boyfriend she told me about or someone new. How could she not be? Even if her personality sucked, *which it didn't*, guys would still be swarming around her because of her incredible allure. It's like leaving a stack of donuts out in the open in a breakroom. Do you know what I mean? Even if you don't know what's on the inside of them, those are still tasty-looking donuts." He looks at me as I chuckle at his comparison. "In all of my years of writing, I never thought I'd compare the love of my life to a donut."

"Donuts are amazing," I agree.

"They really are," he laughs. "You get it."

"I could see why you'd want to distract yourself. Otherwise she would consume your entire life."

"And not just my writing," he agrees. "That's painful enough. Well…" he trails off, "painful might be harsh. It's both painful and exhilarating. I get to visit Anna again anytime I write about a love interest in a story. In that way, I am always revisiting her, creating new opportunities for us, and creating a life for the both of us to share. I get to create happy endings for us." He looks away. The emotion brought about by his memory is clearly getting to him. He so desperately longs to have another chance with Anna. It is a heartbreaking thing to witness. I cannot help but want to support him in some way, but that is the kicker – no one can help him. Suddenly, Wade catches himself staring off and returns to our conversation. "So, yeah, despite my reputation, I may not be the lady killer you'd expect, but I can still give you a tip."

"Please," I accept.

"Find one thing about…?"

"Brianna."

"...Brianna that is small. Something that no one else would even think to mention. But it has to be something you love – drives you mad. Focus in on that thing and explain why you love it."

"Do you mean something physical or emotional?"

"It doesn't matter. You can probably tie the two together."

"What do I do after that?"

"You let her know," he says simply. "You let her know that every small thing about her moves you."

"I know something," I think aloud.

"Go for it," he says.

"She has these two small freckles on the side of her mouth. They're almost microscopic. They're impossible to see unless you're up close. Like *really* up close. But that's what I like about them. They're a reward for getting close to her. And that has been my biggest accomplishment in life so far. I have been able to get close to her, both physically and emotionally. Her every nuance and 'imperfection' fascinates me. They give her even deeper beauty than I thought possible."

Wade smiles. "That's good. She's lucky to have you."

"I don't know about that."

"No, I'm serious. Only true love could bring about a sentiment like that."

I pause before asking my next question, but I have to ask it. The perfect segue was just offered to me. "The way you wrote about 'Anna' was eerie to me."

"How so?" he asks.

"It felt so real. I honestly felt as though you had met Brianna and you guys had previously had an affair behind my back."

"I can assure you that didn't happen," he laughs. "I'm a bit older than you."

"I wouldn't have even minded, though. That's the crazy thing. I would've been so happy that someone did justice to how I felt about Brianna. That someone else saw what I see in her."

"Well, that's a weird way to compliment my writing – accusing me of cheating with your girlfriend – but thanks, Guy."

"You said only true love could bring about sentiment like the way I described her."

"Yeah, I did."

"Well, if I felt that way when reading about Anna, then...?"

"What?"

"Did you love her?"

35

"Did I love Anna?" Wade restates. "That's what you're asking me?"

"You said if I was truthful to you, then you would be truthful to me," I reply.

"I did say that."

"And I was."

"You were."

"So?"

Wade takes a breath. "You shouldn't pursue a career as a movie director, Guy."

"Why not?"

"You're much more suited as a therapist. I can tell. It takes a certain skillset to get people to divulge intimate details the way you do."

I smile. "Thanks, I guess."

"Do you know why I came here tonight?" Wade asks. "To leave the glorious privacy of my home and see a movie that I have literally seen dozens of times?"

"No, why?"

"*Goodfellas* is my favorite movie, but it was also *her* favorite movie. I wrote about our shared love of that movie in my book. What's also true about my book is that we only spent one night together. We never got to share other moments with each other, like eating our favorite dinners, taking drives to our favorite spots, or even watching this – our favorite movie – together. I wish we had, but that never happened. So, I do the things that remind me of her, like coming here tonight. It refreshes my memory of her."

In that moment, Wade's anguish is apparent.

"How long has it been since you've seen her?"

"I still dream about her every single night. Part of me loves it because it's the only time I get to see her – to experience her beauty all over again. But part of me hates it because it means I'll never get over her, and my pain will never cease."

"So, you haven't actually seen each other in person for a while?" I ask, disappointed.

"Basically two years. As time goes by, despite my dreams, I find it more and more difficult to visualize her in the way I once did. Sure, I know the words I wrote. Those will last forever. But I want to be able to see her at will, without referencing my book or those words. I want to be able to visualize her on command. That's why I watch this movie as often as I can. Because when I do, I get to imagine a second date with her. A second chance."

"I had no idea that your book was so literal," I say, astonished.

"It's not literal," he quickly adds. "Not entirely. But the way I felt about her was. *Is*. You can fake scenarios, but you can't fake emotion like that."

I look at Wade, itching to ask him the question – the question he does not want to answer. I know I should not breach his personal life in such a way, but maybe he is right. Maybe I am just a therapist in the making. If so, I need to know the root of all things.

"Go ahead," he says with closed eyes.

"With what?"

"Your next question."

"You sure?"

"No, but yes."

I take a breath. "Who was Anna?"

He shakes his head. I am not sure why. It seems as though he is battling an internal demon. One that has taken hold of his life. "She's exactly who I said she was."

"Is she real?"

"Of course she is," he scoffs. "Like I just said, you can't fake emotion like that."

"Was that her real name?"

"No."

"Have you heard from her?"

He tilts his head to the side. "Do you really want to know the truth?"

"I really do."

"Once you know the magic of the movies, the illusion is forever broken."

"I want it to be broken."

Wade smiles, but the smile is pained. "I'm asked this a lot – more than anything else. Even more than the suicide questions raised from my first book. But the truth is, I would take away readers' enjoyment of the story if I did reveal everything. You can understand that, right?"

"I understand," I acknowledge.

"And based on my answer," he elaborates further, "a person could alter his or her own love life."

"I don't think I follow," I say, struggling to keep up.

"Based on what I say, a person might make alterations to his own love life. He might find bravery, or worse, find cowardice. You know what I mean? That's a heavy thing. If I say anything is possible, that love can thrive, then a man might sweep the woman he loves off her feet and live happily ever after. It's like what you and I did earlier."

"What we did?"

"Yeah, when I had you name something small about Brianna that you loved. You believed me when I said you could sweep her off her feet by telling her that thing the next time you see her."

"You weren't being honest?"

"Of course I was, but that's the point. If I conversely said that true love isn't possible, then maybe you wouldn't have found that small thing about Brianna and held onto it and acknowledged it in the way you did. Maybe you would have become cynical about love."

"I can see your point."

"So when people ask me about my love for 'Anna,' it's a lot more complicated than the black-and-white question being asked. I want everyone to feel that kind of love in their lives. The kind I felt – *feel* – for her. But if I divulge every truth about what happened, then that may sour someone else's life. That wouldn't be fair."

"And the best authors are the ones who are truthful."

"Exactly," he says pointing at me. "So what am I supposed to say? That I wrote the ultimate love letter to the love of my life and she never acknowledged it? That I've never heard from her since that night on the beach? No one wants to hear that."

"Is that true?" I ask.

"Does it matter?"

"If it is true, then maybe it's because she doesn't know about the book? Or maybe she doesn't know it's about her?"

"Or maybe she does, and she's being my 'Petrarchan' love for life," he quickly adds. "Maybe she knows *exactly* what she's doing. That by not acknowledging my love, she is preserving my ability to write about her forever. To make herself my muse forever."

"That is... both sad and incredible," I say. "If it's true."

"What I do know," Wade continues, "is that book would have swept any other girl off her feet. She would've been mine forever. Followed me anywhere, as you said. But not my Anna. And that's what makes her my 'Petrarchan Girl.'"

"Have you tried to contact her since?"

"Never got her number."

"Seriously?"

"I travel all over the country. In the evening, when the sun sets, I always leave my hotel room and walk around the city or town that I'm in and look for her. By all accounts, she's either in Florida or Maine, and yet I'll look for her every place I go. Even here in small-town Missouri. I know it's ridiculous. It's impossible for her to be here, and yet I desperately look nonetheless. I just imagine stumbling upon her one night, in her unassuming way, ready to begin a life with me. She's a lot like Annie Hall. Do you know that movie?"

"One of my favorites."

"My time with her was incredibly limited, and yet the story of my life revolves around meeting her. She completely changed my life in such a short amount of time."

"How does it make you feel when people say *Petrarchan Girl* is their favorite book of yours?"

Wade chuckles. "Sad but good at the same time. I'm glad my open-heart wound has inspired my devout readers, but I can't help but think that the story deserved a better ending in my own personal life."

"You're a weird guy," I say boldly to Wade.

"Oh, yeah?" he smiles.

"You made me believe that true love is only attainable through heartache. That's a weird notion."

He smiles. "It's weird like most true things are."

"What advice do you have for someone about to begin life after high school?" I ask. It is the first time I actually sound like I am writing a student paper.

"Find what you're passionate about and pursue it, whether it's a profession or a person," he responds. "And if possible, find a way to reconcile the two. That's what life is all about – remaining vital."

"You're the most successful person I've interviewed so far, so I'll definitely take that advice."

"Let me be clear, though," Wade adds. "Success does not equal happiness. Take it from me. I had the biggest success of my life two years ago and my life has, by all accounts, gotten worse in every way, except financially. I don't care about that, though. Love is the most important thing. Love and passion."

"Well, it seems as though you still have a passion burning inside of you. Maybe you'll find another love as well someday," I say boldly. I then remember his earlier comment about his current relationship, so I quickly add, "If you haven't already."

"Love," he says with a soft chuckle. He slowly bends his neck so that he is looking at the ceiling. My comment has clearly triggered the "author" side of his brain. "I may have said that word in the past, and perhaps I will say it in the future to someone else, but I was never more honest than when I directed that word at her."

I think deeply about whether I should ask my next question or not. I do not want to offend him, but I am really curious as to how he would answer me. I feel like I am in a *real* moment with Wade now, however, so it is now or never. "Do you think you'll ever write about anyone else? You may never love anyone like you loved Anna, but surely you will find someone else who is interesting enough to write about, romantically speaking. Don't you think?"

"Based on your screening of *Touch of Evil* tonight, I know you show a lot of older films," Wade begins. "Have you ever screened the film *Rebecca*, from the 1940s?"

"Yeah, we did a few years ago," I answer. "My parents are big Hitchcock fans."

"Maybe you'll remember this moment, or maybe you won't, but there is a line in that movie which answers your question perfectly. At the very beginning of *Rebecca*, Laurence Olivier is asking Joan Fontaine about her upbringing, and he asks what he father did for a living. She tells him that her father was a painter, but that he was always misunderstood. When asked why, she says that her father painted nature scenes – but with only *one* particular tree as the focal point. Her father's advice was this: If you find one perfect thing, place, or person, then you should stick with it. That's why he only painted that one perfect tree his entire life." Wade allows me a moment to absorb his analogy and to reach the conclusion he desires. "That's exactly how I feel about Anna. I don't ever want to write about anyone else."

"What are you going to do now?" I ask him, steering the conversation somewhere new. He looks grateful.

"Well, right now, I'm going to go home to rest. I've got a big day ahead of me tomorrow. I'm flying down to Florida."

"Oh yeah?" I ask excitedly, anticipating the reason.

"Yeah," he smiles. "I still go down there often. Just in case."

He stands up to leave but I stop him before he gets away. "Hey, Wade?"

"Yeah?" he answers over his shoulder.

"I know that in the future you will probably write in other genres and about different subjects…" I start.

"Go on," he encourages.

"Don't stop writing about her."

"Why? You want a sequel?" he laughs.

"No," I chuckle. "It's just that... when you write about her, it helps me realize what it is I love about Brianna. You seem to understand my feelings better than anybody else. Maybe it's because you're from around here and I relate to you in that way. I don't know."

"That's not why," he shakes his head. "Love is universal. It's because you love her."

I smile. "You're right."

"Don't worry," Wade says as he places his hand on the door to leave, "I couldn't stop writing about Anna if I tried."

36

When I enter the theater lobby, I see Caitlyn and Kylie fixated on Wade's exit. I can tell he had a short chat with them as he left, and they look more than happy with their brief encounter. Once Wade is out the door, they rush over to me.

"Kylie, what are you doing back here? I thought you were grounded when you aren't scheduled to work?"

"I am."

"So?"

"I snuck out. Big deal. I do it all the time."

My head falls onto the back of my shoulders. *Some people you just can't reach.* And then the questions begin –

"How'd it go?"

"What was he like?"

"Did he talk about her?"

"Is he with Anna?"

I shake my head at the barrage. "You guys act like he's some sort of Don Juan or something."

"Huh?" both say in unison.

"Dirk Diggler?" I try. "Is that better?" Caitlyn doesn't get the reference, but Kylie, unsurprisingly, does.

"Any person who can write the way he did about Anna deserves…" Caitlyn trails off.

"Deserves what?" I ask.

She sighs. "I don't know. Whatever he wants."

"I think you'd be surprised about the life he actually lives," I say.

"What do you mean?" Kylie asks. "He's not swimming in it?"

"I'm not sure about his swimming conditions – he didn't say – but I think the idea of 'Anna' was… just that. An idea."

Both girls fall silent. "She's not real?" Kylie scoffs.

"No, she's real, but I don't think his novel was meant to be read like a textbook. You know how some painters use a photograph as a reference point for their work? Well, I think Wade took some significant liberties when he painted his picture."

"So Wade's just like us – unhappy?" Kylie scoffs even more.

"Again, I'm not his therapist, but I think his life resembles our everyday lives a bit more than we'd like to imagine."

"What's the point then?"

"What do you mean?"

"I mean, if he can't find happiness – with Anna or whoever – then what chance do we have? He had legit *emotion* for her, ya know?"

"I know what you mean, but I don't think every story has to have a happy ending."

"It would be nice if some did," Caitlyn mumbles.

"And I don't think Wade's ending is unhappy, necessarily."

"What do you mean?" Caitlyn asks with renewed hope.

"He told me right before he left that he looks for Anna everywhere, even in the most obscure places and towns."

"Um... okay?" Kylie says, unsatisfied.

"The point is that he's still looking for her," I say. "She gave him hope... something to drive him. Even if they didn't end up together, she gave him the will to live and write. That's huge."

"It's not very sexy," Kylie says, rolling her eyes.

"No, it isn't," I agree, "but it's more realistic. I think it's an even better ending."

Caitlyn and Kylie both groan.

"You're an idiot," Kylie says.

"I don't usually agree with Kylie, but she is right on this one," Caitlyn agrees. "The point of books and movies is escapism, Guy. We want to leave our crappy lives and find hope in someone else's story. Why would I want to read about the misery that always surrounds us as it is? How is that a better ending?"

"Because it's truthful," I insist. "Truth is always better. It's tougher, sure, but it's more satisfying. Like medicine."

"I'm sorry," Kylie interrupts, holding her hand up to my face, "but did you just compare true love with Tylenol? You are such a loser. For reals. Thank God you weren't the author of *Petrarchan Girl*. Imagine the kind of nonsense you'd end that story on. 'He returned to Florida to find...'"

"'...only a rising tide,'" Caitlyn adds to the story.

"'And seeing nothing but the great expanse of water – no Anna, no future...'"

"'...he did the only thing he could do. The thing he was *born* to do.'"

"'He walked out into the ocean and accepted his fate.'"

"'He walked and walked, until his toes could no longer grip the sand beneath his feet.'"

"'Once there was nothing beneath him, he let out what was left in him…'"

"'His will to live.'"

"'And the air in his body.'"

"'Oh, yeah, and the air in his body, of course.'"

"'Once those two things were absent from him…'"

"'He sank down into the deep water, with the ocean floor nowhere in sight.'"

"'As he sank, he looked up to the sky above the water. The sun's rays rippled against the waves, but they grew dimmer and dimmer, just as his love for Anna did.'"

"'And just as love escaped him, so did the sun. And when it did…'"

"'He died.'"

"'He totally died.'"

I stare at the two aspiring authors before me. "Wow, that was really… inspiring. You really need to work on that ending, though. It didn't satisfy the buildup."

"We'll workshop it," Caitlyn smiles.

We all laugh at the absurdity of the moment and of life in general, I suppose.

"Maybe you're right," I finally agree. "Maybe the 'happy' ending is the better one."

37

As the three of us walk to our respective cars, we say our usual goodbyes. Kylie is the first to get into her car. She is always more than happy to leave this place. Plus, she is grounded, of course. When she starts her car up, gangster rap explodes from her speakers. As she passes us, she rolls down her window and does an impromptu dance out of the car's window, steering the car with her leg.

"Would you just get out of here?" I laugh.

"Drive safe!" Caitlyn shouts over the music.

Kylie flips us off, smiles, and spins out of the parking lot. Normally that gesture is offensive, but it is her traditional goodbye. It is how she spreads her love.

"Do you have the next 'double' figured out yet?" Caitlyn asks as she puts the key into her car door. She drives a beater, like everyone else our age around here does, but her beater is in much better condition than the rest of ours. Kind of like Caitlyn herself.

"I have one movie in mind that I'd like to screen, but I don't know what to pair it with," I say, opening my car door.

"Maybe I can help?" she suggests.

Until Caitlyn's last suggestion about my planned *Hud/Whiplash* double, no one has ever helped me decide the lineup of one of our double features before, but nothing about the past few months has been "normal" either. *Her input last time did seem to work out pretty well…*

"Yeah, okay," I say. "I would like to find something to pair with *A Star is Born*."

"The new one that just came out?"

"Yeah."

"You never choose movies that are *that* new. Why that one?"

"I'm not sure. Something about it really hit me when we screened it opening weekend last year. I actually watched it twice that day, and I never do that."

"Yeah, that's unusual for you. Why do you think that was?"

"I'm honestly still not sure. It's typically not my type of movie at all, but I still find myself drawn to it."

She hesitates. "You're not suicidal, are you? I mean, it's okay if you are... Well, not *okay*, but what I mean is I can get you help... Not like a psych ward or... Do they still call them that? Was I using an offensive term? I don't want to ship you off anywhere. What I meant to say was..." she trails off.

I wait for her to finish her incoherent thoughts. "What?"

"I'm here for you. I'd be more than happy to listen to you if you need someone to... listen to you."

I cannot help but smile at her pure kindness. "No, I'm not suicidal. Not at all."

"Thank God," she exhales.

"I don't think you have to have the problems of a film's characters in order to connect with them, though. So yeah, I'm not sure why I'm drawn to that movie, but that's why I want to screen it again. Maybe I'll understand it better this time. Or... myself."

Caitlyn looks up at the sky and squints an eye. "You definitely have a better knowledge of film than I do. I mean, I just work here because it's local and I need gas money. You work here because it is your entire life, in a way."

"You're not wrong," I agree.

"So I can't tell you what film would *thematically* go with it, or what the 'auteur theory' is, or anything else academic like that. I do, though, have a pretty good handle on emotions, or as much as any teenager can, I suppose."

"I'd also agree with that. You're the most level-headed person our age, by a long shot."

"And while you say you love film because of cinematography and sound design and editing and method acting and everything else, I also think you're being the *slightest* bit ingenuine."

"Ingenuine? Me?" I say with mock offense as if I were Kenneth Branagh performing *Hamlet*.

"Yes, just a little bit," she laughs. "I think you're drawn to movies because of the emotion they rile up in you. You feel like you're stuck – in this town, with these people, in this building, with this life. You want to feel something unusual and exciting. You want to live vicariously through someone else, maybe not for a lifetime, but definitely for two hours."

Caitlyn is hitting a bit too close to my actual feelings, so I do what any man of my age does in this situation – I clam up.

"If you want this next double to be special, and I know you do because it's the last one scheduled before our graduation *and* our last one together as a group, then you need to just dig deep. Don't overthink it."

"How do I dig deep and not overthink it at the same time?"

"Get into your feels, Guy," Caitlyn smiles.

"And how would one go about that?" I chuckle uneasily.

"Bring up the playlist."

"Playlist?"

"*The* playlist."

"What playlist?"

"Guy, everyone has a playlist on their phone that they cue up anytime they want to feel emo when they're lying in bed at night. When you want to feel both angry and sad and maybe even cry…" she stops when she sees my face contort. "Well, maybe not *cry*, but when you feel like you don't understand why your life is going the way it is. *That* playlist."

We blankly stare at each other.

"Do you have such a playlist, Guy?"

A pause.

"Maybe."

"Bring it up tonight as you're going to bed. Close your eyes and completely devote yourself to the music. Think of nothing else. As soon as it's over, or as you're about to fall asleep, turn it off and choose the first movie that comes to mind. That's how you simultaneously dig deep without overthinking. Okay?"

I feel the conversation surround me at this moment as though it were a physical presence. It is uncomfortable, and I wish to escape it immediately.

"Okay," I agree.

With that, Caitlyn and I get into our cars and drive away from the building that seems to be defining my life more and more each day.

PART SIX

VERTIGO

A STAR IS BORN

38

"Are you ready?!"

Kylie comes running down the lobby stairs. She is thrilled that tonight is our last night working together at the Bristol Arts Theater. Our class, the class of 2019, graduates on Sunday, a mere two days from now. Kylie already has plans to leave town that night and begin her life of adventure. I, on the other hand, am not as excited to get shot out of life's gun just yet. And while I have not been able to get Caitlyn to confide in me, I can tell she is more in the Kylie camp.

"Last one," I acknowledge.

"You're not gonna get all sentimental and shit, are you?" she goads.

"No," I huff like a grade-schooler. *I totally was.*

"Good, because we should be excited about tonight!" Kylie continues. "This is the beginning of it all!"

"And the end," I mumble strictly to myself.

Just then, Caitlyn comes through the side door to join us. She takes one look at Kylie's face and impeccably reads the room. "She's already celebrating, isn't she?"

Kylie runs over to Caitlyn. Kylie's hands cup the sides of Caitlyn's face, fully invading her personal space. "I wuv you so much," she says as she squishes Caitlyn's face. "Yur such a purty gurl. Has anyone told you that lately?" She continues to contort Caitlyn's face. "I just want you to be happy, too."

Caitlyn pulls away, equal parts humored and annoyed. "I am happy, you moron. You didn't even give me a chance to fully get in the door."

See? You're the only one.

Shut up.

Just be happy. For them. You can fake it, right?

I usually do.

Well, do it again.

"Well?" Kylie says approximately two feet from my face, arms crossed.

I stare back blankly. "Well, what?"

"I'd really like to know what goes on in your head, sometimes," she shakes her head.

No, you wouldn't.

Maybe you should give her a chance.

Shut up.

You never give anyone a chance.

Shut up!

You're such a...

"Hey!" Kylie shouts.

"I'm sorry," I reply, shaking my head as if it will rattle away my thoughts. "What did you say?"

"I *said*, are we still doing the thing? The lonely boy writes a fake essay for college thing?"

"Yes, I recall what you're talking about, Kylie. Thank you. And yeah, I planned on it. One last time."

One more.

"Lot of pressure tonight," Caitlyn says as she steps back into our conversation circle. The crowd for tonight's double feature has been slowly trickling in. I had not paid much attention to our arriving customers, but apparently Caitlyn is already on top of things.

"I guess so," I shrug. "I just have to come up with a good ending to my 'essay.' I have to find some sort of answer to it all."

"Do you know where it's leading yet?" Caitlyn asks. Kylie now steps away from our circle and peers into the auditorium.

"Not really," I admit. "But I'm just going to go with my gut. Like you suggested."

I catch Kylie slyly making eye contact with Caitlyn before she returns to us.

"I think that's how most good stories unravel," Caitlyn suggests. "You don't necessarily need to have an ending in mind. You just have to arrive at a point when you get there."

"So are you actually writing an essay?" Kylie asks. "I mean, I know your whole story is b.s., but have you thought about it?"

"Thought about writing an essay?"

"Yeah, just to go over what you learned from every person you talked to. It might be interesting."

"Maybe that's when you'll find your ending?" Caitlyn adds.

"I hadn't really thought about it," I answer. "To be honest, the thought of writing an essay, or whatever, during the first summer after our high school graduation kinda sounds like a huge bummer. Why would I want to do 'school work' when I'm no longer required to?"

"It would be *because* you're no longer required to," Caitlyn says. "I think you can find meaning in doing something when you're not forced to."

I shrug at the thought. *Who knows?*

I doubt it.

"Do you need to go scope out the crowd some more, Kyle?" I ask. "We have about ten minutes before the first feature."

"Already did."

"You already found someone?"

"I did."

"Okay…?"

She stares blankly back at me.

"Well? Do you have any information for me?"

"I already told Cate my choice. She knows who to go after."

"I do," she says. "In fact, I'm going in now."

"You're going in now? This soon, before the first movie even starts? That's not how we…" I end up finishing my sentence to empty air. Kylie just smiles at me. "What's so funny? Is the person some sort of 'Quasimodo'?"

"Well, that was mean."

"You know what I'm saying. You're just gawking at me like a grandmother waiting for me to open a Christmas gift."

"Quasimodo was a nice man."

"I know…"

"He was unfairly hated by the town."

"I *know*…"

"He was a hero, Guy."

"I know! Sorry, I didn't mean to... hunch-back shame, or whatever."

Caitlyn returns to our group. "She's in."

"Okay, finally we have some good information," I say, breathing a sigh of relief.

"Guy was just asking about the person," Kylie updates her. "He thinks she's some sort of monster."

"Hardly," Caitlyn shakes her head.

"Okay, well can I get a description then? I need to know who to look for between movies."

"Oh no," Caitlyn stops me. "You're going in now."

"I am?"

"You are."

"And she knows this?"

"She does."

"No roof?"

"No roof."

Suddenly, I am filled with anxiety. *This is my last "report" – my last interview. What if it goes poorly? What if I don't know what to say? What if I don't end up learning what I need to know? What if this all leads to failure? What if my life becomes a failure?*

I try to collect myself. "Okay, I can do this."

"You can do this," Kylie and Caitlyn agree in unison.

"Thank you," I nod. "I'll do it. I'm going in."

I push open the door to the auditorium when suddenly Caitlyn says, "Don't you want to know who to look for?"

I stop in my tracks and turn my head. "Oh, yeah. Okay, what does she look like?"

"You're going to want to go to the back of the theater and to the right side."

"Okay, got it. Physical attributes?"

"You can't miss her. She's currently sitting alone. She's a knock-out."

Seems fishy. A "knock-out" sitting alone? "Okay, what else?"

"She is wearing a Harlan High School tee shirt and cut-off jean shorts. She has dark hair and incredible legs. But mostly, you're going to notice her eyes. They pierce through the darkness."

39

"Hey, Guy."

Brianna looks up at me and pats the seat next to her.

"I should've known," I say.

"So what's this I hear about a college essay?" she squints at me good naturedly.

"It's a long story," I say, somewhat embarrassed. "I'll fill you in."

Just then the Bernard Herrmann score of Alfred Hitchcock's *Vertigo* kicks in. The house lights go down.

"Let's wait for the intermission," I say. I can tell she wants more elaborate answers, to everything, but the movie saves me. I have some time to reconcile my thoughts.

How do I explain all of this to her?

You should've done it long ago.

Regardless, Brianna accepts my answer without any hesitation. In fact, I think she is thoroughly interested in what exactly her boyfriend has been up to. She is curious about the mystery of it all. I know this to be true because she bends herself down under my arm and snuggles herself into my body.

"You really thought that talking to strangers could help prepare you for life outside of high school? You don't even know these people, Guy. Everyone's life circumstances are different. They may not pertain to you or the life you're going to lead."

"They may not, but they may. That's the whole point."

"Why do it during movies?"

"My life basically takes place here at this theater. It's my whole life."

"I know, but why on double-feature night, once a month?"

"Based on my experience here, the double features bring out more unusual people. Yes, the regulars still come, but the doubles also bring people who only occasionally drop in. My odds of getting an interesting person were higher. There's something special about these nights."

"Did you find some interesting people?"

"I did."

Brianna pauses to think. So many questions remain about my crazy scenario and, frankly, mindset. Since she is my girlfriend, I can only imagine that she is also probably hurt that I have kept her out of the loop for so long.

"Why did you choose *Vertigo*?"

"I wasn't sure what movie to pick, so I asked Caitlyn for help. She told me to go with my gut. And it actually kind of worked."

"How so?"

"Because of you. I didn't know you were going to be my last loner…"

"'Loner'?"

"Yeah, that's what we called them – the people I have been interviewing. Anyway, I didn't think it would be you, but now I realize it totally makes sense."

"Are you wanting to throw me off a rooftop or something?"

"Not at all," I laugh. "Quite the opposite."

"Do tell," she leans in, putting her chin on top of her closed fist while her arm plants itself on the armrest. I do not know why, but it is the sexiest look I can imagine.

"Well, obviously I'm not Hitchcock…"

"Obviously. You haven't had your post-high school weight gain yet."

"Exactly," I laugh. "Even still, I think I know what this movie is about."

"What's it about, in your estimation?"

"It's about the literal sensations of love. How… physical love can develop, or how it can manifest itself."

"Yeah, but the movie almost makes it seem like love is impossible."

"Yeah, it does," I agree. "The movie also makes love seem as though it's almost dangerous, too. I mean, Jimmy Stewart practically stalked that woman before making her become his lost love, both emotionally and physically."

"But it's the same girl," Brianna says. "Madeline and Judy are the same person."

"I know, but he doesn't realize it at first. He just gets that overwhelming emotional feeling, without having any evidence. It all comes down to that scene when he first sees Madeline."

"You mean in the restaurant?"

I nod. "Do you remember how the scene is filmed when Scottie first spots her? He doesn't even fully see her. He just sees her profile. There's that great close-up of Kim

Novak in the bright green dress, with her blonde hair, against the red background."

"Right. And the background kind of became blurry."

"It goes out of focus to highlight the beauty Scottie sees in her. The red back-drop suddenly pops and blends into itself, creating one moving, almost hallucinatory image. And Scottie's just stuck there at the bar. He can't move. He can't even look at her head-on. He can only use his peripheral vision to take her in, and even that seems too much for him. He is overcome with his sudden desire for her. It's almost violent in its urgency."

"It's a great shot in the movie, and it's a great sentiment you're expressing, but I'm still not sure I understand. Why does that make this the perfect movie for tonight?"

I am almost taken aback by her lack of understanding. "That's how I feel every day when I see you again for the first time." I take a moment to really look at Brianna, to understand how lucky I am to have her. Thinking about Wade's advice, I look at her small freckles. "In that scene, Scottie's seed of desire is born, and that's when mine is, too. Each day you reappear in my life – each day I get the privilege of seeing my favorite person enter the room I'm in – my life changes."

Brianna leans in and kisses me deeply. I did not spout my explanation just to earn her physical affection (although it is always nice and appreciated). I did it because it was my realized truth.

She kisses me passionately, unaware of those around us. It is not a conciliatory kiss, either. Most couples get to that stage by year two or three, from my observations of both movies and moviegoers. The act of kissing becomes more about the idea of "Yes, I still love you and this is how society accepts that display. I kiss you, for roughly two seconds, and you, my love, must feel placated and admired for the time being. That all changes when we get home, of course, but for the time being, here is a kiss so that we can keep our relationship going another six months." It is more of an oil change than true affection.

This, however, is not that kind of kiss, because Brianna is not that kind of woman. She feels and exudes passion. She has no sense of acting in her. If she does not feel love, she will not show love. She does not "grin and bear it" for anyone, least of all for some dopey, teenage male who is facing his first existential crisis.

Brianna pulls away and really speaks to me. "I haven't felt close to you in some time."

"I know."

"Can you tell me why?"

"It's hard to put into words," I sigh.

She holds my head in her hands. "When I don't feel close to you, I don't feel close to anyone. I need you to try to explain."

I have mere seconds to condense my thoughts—
Time is limited, running out.
I'm aware of that fact and yet I'm ignoring you.
In fact, I'm almost rude to you. I'm giving my focus to others.
Why?
Is it some sort of self-imposed jealousy?
Would I feel better if you chose me and didn't leave?
No, I would be left with guilt.

You cannot give up a bright, opportune life for me.
I'm literally doing everything I shouldn't be doing.
I should be focusing only on you.
Spending time with you. Connecting. Talking.
But something hangs overhead.
The inevitable is still inevitable.
Time is running out.
I'm doing it all wrong.
Now, you resent me and won't feel bad about leaving.
What a joke I am.

"Well?" she prompts again.

"I want to blame something or someone for my actions. I want to have a villain. But there is no villain, because this is real life. Villains are for those who need an excuse for the harsh realities of life."

"Then take responsibility," she says. "Tell me what it is you need to tell me."

The Warner Brothers logo appears onscreen as the lights go down once again. There is no trumpet fanfare this time.

"I think I can, but I may be able to explain my thoughts better if I have time to try to understand them myself."

"How much time do you need?" she asks, visibly annoyed.

"Two hours?" I gesture toward the screen.

She turns forward in her seat and I do the same.

I have two hours to make sense of all of this turmoil.

Two hours to tell her what it is I really feel about her.

Two hours to save our relationship.

40

"Don't wanna feel another touch
Don't wanna start another fire
Don't wanna know another kiss
Don't wanna give my heart away
To another stranger"

A Star is Born ends and Brianna is openly weeping. I am crying, too, but not openly. I try to suck my tears back into my eyes by looking at the ceiling, hoping that they will recede from whence they came.

"Please don't tell me you're Jackson Maine," she says while wiping tears from her eyes. "I certainly know I'm not Ally."

I try to shake off any open emotions left over from the film, which is more than difficult. "I think you are, though."

"You're so dramatic. I love you, but you don't seem to have a real handle on what is fiction or reality in life."

"I told you I would have an answer for you. Why I have been acting the way I have."

"Do you have an answer now?"

"I do."

She breathes deeply. The patrons around us exit while we dissect the state of our relationship. "Give it to me."

"So the scene in the movie…"

"Here we go."

"No, hold on a second."

She cannot help but look disappointed, but she still humors me. "Okay."

"You know the scene in the movie where Ally takes the stage for the first time?" I begin.

"They sing 'Shallow.' Yeah, it's probably the most memorable part of the whole movie."

"I think I know why. And it relates to how I feel right now, on the cusp of graduation."

"I'm listening."

I begin my explanation. "Jackson is already an established star at that point. He has a great career. Sure, it ebbs and flows, but he's touring and has a fanbase. But he knows Ally, the woman he's falling in love with, has something special in her. She is maybe even more special than he is himself. He's eager to unleash her, but deep down, he also knows what that'll mean for him."

"I think you're confused. He's more than happy to have her onstage. He's in love with her."

"He is, but he knows that his career will dim once she steps into the spotlight. She is about to outshine him. Her career is going to explode. He will become the celebrity musician husband."

"What's wrong with that?"

"Nothing inherently. In fact, he's more than happy to do it. He is so enamored with Ally and her abilities that he creates her celebrity. But there's also no turning back after that. Once Ally takes hold of her great capabilities in life, Jack loses grip on his. Ally is too big for the both of them."

"So it's her fault that he has a downward spiral?"

"Not at all. Their lives just change because she shows promise. She is capable. Their love changes."

"I think I'm beginning to understand now," Brianna shakes her head.

"It's the same lesson in *Vertigo*. Love is dangerous because it cannot be sustained if it is too real, passionate, or all-consuming."

I think back to our kiss after the last movie.

"You think that about us?" she asks. "That our love cannot be sustained?"

"I just don't know," I shrug. "I mean, how can it? You're leaving in a matter of weeks. It's kind of hard for passion to sustain itself in that kind of environment. And just look at you."

Brianna scrunches her face as she looks down at herself. "Guy, I'm in a jank tee shirt and cut-off shorts."

"Exactly. And look how stunning you are. You exude the most extreme kind of beauty even when you don't try. I can't compete with that." I look around at our environment – the now-empty movie auditorium. "I'm just a high school grad, stuck in the same town he grew up in, running a business that is sure to die at any point. My life begins and ends in the exact same spot."

"So, finally, it all comes out. That's what this is all about… you're worried that your life is going to stall out? That you're not good enough for me? That you're gonna be forgotten? Is that it?"

"Basically," is all I can come up with.

"If you were so concerned about our lives after high school, why didn't you just talk it out with me. You know, like a normal person? Instead, you go to a bunch of 'loners' and dissect their life stories in an attempt to figure out why our relationship and your future can't coincide." She pauses to examine everything she just summed up. "That's really kind of messed up, Guy."

"I know," I say. I lean back in my chair.

"Life isn't a movie," she says as I look at the blank screen. "You realize that, right?"

"I do."

"This is what you do, though," she continues. "You concoct these wild scenarios and try to figure out an ending as if you're workshopping a screenplay."

"I don't think they're wild scenarios, though. You *really* are going off to college without me. Moving to a different city. I *really* am staying here, in this same town. I *really* am going to run this movie theater for my retiring parents. These are all *real* facts in my life."

"So what's the ending for the story of us? Both of the movies tonight ended in the death of one of the loved ones. Is that what you see happening?"

"Not an untimely death, no."

"Well, that's reassuring."

"I think I need to workshop it some more."

She presses on. "Give me the unfinished version. The original author's version. *Your* version."

I take a breath. "I see us continuing our relationship for the next few months, maybe even a year. But then you will find someone who also lives on campus. He'll have ambition and drive. He'll be attractive, of course. After flirting for a while during daily study sessions at the library, you'll cement your mutual desires with a kiss over an anthropology textbook. You'll feel guilty, yet excited, as you nearly sprint back to your dorm room that night. You'll need to figure out how to handle this new, delicate situation. So the communications between us will dwindle as the communications between you and the attractive college student increase. Before long, our break-up will be no more painful than receiving a parking ticket you know you deserved. Your relationship with the new man may continue on after you receive your degree, or it may not, but that's not the point. Once you're rid of me – your high school love, the hardest one to overcome early in life – it'll become much easier for you to navigate future relationships. You'll fully understand what you want in a boyfriend by then, and you'll go after that. What you won't want is your townie, high school boyfriend whose life goals are to keep a crumbling building alive and live for the weekends."

I take a breath after unleashing the harsh realities.

"Anything else?" she asks.

"None of this is bad for you, though. You're going to be a very successful person, with a legitimate career and loving family. You will because that's the kind of person you are. That's what you deserve."

Brianna has been staring at me throughout my spiel, but she looks away when I am finished. "I can tell that you have orchestrated that scenario for a long time now, Guy."

"It's hard not to dwell on my fears."

She turns her attention toward me again. "Couples only make it if they are able to communicate with each other. Open up to one another. To be honest, yet still loving. You can't script out our lives without any input from me. I'm the overbearing leading actress. I don't sign onto any film without script approval."

That makes me smile. "Of course, you'll request a producing credit as well, just in case it's nominated for any major awards."

"Why shouldn't I? I deserve it. People are coming out to see the movie because they know I'm in it."

"That's very true. Ugly directors usually aren't the draw."

"I can think of a few ugly directors that can draw an audience," she says.

We take each other in. The silence of the moment is deafening. It is not just the silence of the empty movie theater, but the silence representing the unknown in our lives. We both feel it.

"I'm afraid too, Guy," she says.

"Really?"

"Really."

"Why? You have such a solid plan for yourself for when we leave high school."

"Nothing is really 'solid' for anyone, though. That's the whole thing. That's why everyone makes a big deal out of high school graduations and not college graduations or even job promotions. Everyone feels the exact same thing when they're eighteen years old, I'd imagine."

"And what's that?"

"Big fat uncertainty. About every single thing. And that's scary."

"I didn't realize you felt…" I begin.

"The same as you?" she interrupts. "Yeah, maybe if you took a moment to talk to me, you would've realized how much more we actually have in common."

The noise made by the ceiling fans in the lobby sound louder than the movie we just watched.

"So what do we do now?" I ask.

"We graduate on Sunday," she answers. "After that, we take it a step at a time."

"Right," I say disconcerted.

Brianna grabs my hand. "But we do it together."

I lean in for a kiss as the projector's light illuminating the silver screen finally turns off.

EPILOGUE

CITY LIGHTS

HER

41

While not as successful as the year prior, 2019 is shaping up to be a tremendous year in terms of box office results. Movies, overall, are bringing in huge crowds nearly everywhere. No, the crowds here at the Bristol Arts Theater are not massive, but they are... *sufficient*. Certainly sufficient enough to keep us alive a bit longer.

I am officially running the theater as manager now, in all but title. Ronnie and Margie are still on-hand as well, but that is it in terms of the old crew. Caitlyn and Kylie both set off on their own journeys. Cate, as expected, seems to be succeeding in her studies. Kylie, on the other hand, seems to be having the time of her life in New York City, at least according to social media. Unlike Cate, Kylie's focus seems to be on partying, dating, obtaining followers, and more partying. So basically, it is high school 2.0 for her.

New to the Bristol's staff are Blake and Danielle. They are both juniors at Hudson High School. While I am still close to them age-wise, I cannot help but feel they are a tremendous step down in maturity from our previous crew. That is saying a lot, considering that Kylie was a part of that last crew. I mark it up to the fact that this is the first job either of them has had, and that is just how it goes. The Bristol is the jumping-off point for most of its high-schooled employees. Most, but not all.

The biggest draw at the theater remains the double-feature program. In fact, it has only grown in popularity this year. The buzz for next month's double of Stanley Kubrick's

A Clockwork Orange and Terry Gilliam's *Fear and Loathing in Las* Vegas has already began on social media and in pre-sales, probably because it appeals to two reliable fan bases – cinephiles and stoner townies – who both always seem to come out for our showings of cult classics. Lord knows what damage would be incurred by our theater if we actually screened the *Evil Dead* trilogy. Tonight, however, we are running Charlie Chaplin's *City Lights* and Spike Jonze's *Her*. A keen viewer can probably point out the common theme pretty simply.

"Hey, Guy," Blake shouts at me as he enters through the front door. "There's a package here for you."

"Probably posters," I shout back, just as obnoxiously, without looking. "Just toss 'em on the desk upstairs."

"This isn't a poster tube," he says.

I turn around and see Blake inspecting the package as though it were a skillfully disguised bomb and he was the captain of the *Hurt Locker* crew. "Here, I'll take it," I say, holding out my hand.

He hands it over gingerly. "Be careful."

I rip it dramatically from his hand as he flinches slightly. From behind the concession counter, Danielle shouts out, "You're such a douche, Flake."

"Hey!" I shout back at her.

"What?" she says, both drawn-out and put-out.

"You can't scream 'douche' in the middle of the lobby, Danielle."

"Why? It's medical."

"I'm going upstairs," I announce. "Take care of the door. Make sure no one slips in without paying. We need all the revenue we can get."

Blake salutes me like a buffoon, and Danielle fully ignores me, giving all her attention to her phone.

I cannot wait to fire them both.

When I finally reach my office upstairs, I sit behind my desk and clear off the posters lying on top. I examine the package's return label.

Wade Parker?

What surprises me most about the package is the timing of its delivery. It is now October of 2019. I interviewed Wade in April. According to local gossip, which is prevalent and practically gospel in Harlan and Hudson, Wade is hard at work on his newest novel. It is kind of surprising that he took the time to send me something. Or that he even remembered me.

I open the yellow, padded envelope and a book slides out into my hand. It is *A Farewell to Arms* by Ernest Hemingway. I have never read it, but based on my studies in high school English, I know that this book takes place during World War I and that it is somewhat based on Hemingway's real-life experiences.

The book is well-worn. Wade probably read it many times himself, I would imagine. I open the hardcover and notice a "Property of Harlan High School" stamp on the first page. He must have lifted it back when he was in school. *Nice.* Below the stamp is an inscription. It reads:

"There's an old joke that goes like this: Why did the chicken cross the road? To die. In the rain. At least that's the answer according to Hemingway."

What a weird way to begin an inscription. It goes on:

"I'm sending you this book, because I wish someone would have given it to me earlier in life. There's a lesson in here, if you're patient and willing enough to find and accept it. I won't spell it all out for you, but I'll say this – something wonderful often comes out of the mess and heartbreak we all face in life.

"Good luck with everything,

"Wade"

I hold onto the book tightly as I return to the lobby downstairs.

"What'd you get, boss?" Blake asks eagerly.

"Nothin', just a book."

Blake bends his neck to read the cover, but quickly disengages when he sees how old it looks.

"Think we'll get many people tonight?" he asks, resuming his duties of sweeping the floor of the entryway.

"Hope not," Danielle mumbles from behind her phone.

"Hard to say," I answer. "The first movie is a silent one, so that may deter some."

"Why would you want to show a silent movie?" she scoffs. "They're miserable. Our history teacher made us watch one."

"What was it called?" I ask.

"I dunno, but it was about the KKK or something."

"Ohh," I respond knowledgeably. "I want to show this one, *City Lights*, because… it's good. Fantastic, actually. If you gave it a chance, you may even like it, Danielle. It's a love story."

"Not interested," she responds flatly. "Hey, how are things with you and…?"

"Brianna."

"…yeah, her."

"Good," I answer. I do not feel like filling Danielle in on my love life, regardless of how well or not my relationship is going.

Truth is, though, that my relationship with Brianna is indeed going well. Amazingly well, actually. We still speak to each other every day and, to the best of my knowledge, she has not met a hunk in the library. We are totally committed to each other and our joint future. In fact, we already have a five-year plan set in place.

Since she is doing so well in college (and I can only assume that will continue), she will undoubtedly land a job as soon as she gets her diploma and starts applying. I, too, seem to be doing surprisingly well. The movie theater, against all odds, is doing great business. It seems as though the interest created by our unique double feature line-ups has generated interest in our old theater overall. My parents could not be more proud of my success and, frankly, neither can I.

I did not expect to do well after high school. I expected my life to immediately drop into the shitter. But for some reason, it has not. I have decided not to question it too much. I give a lot of credit to Brianna, though. She has been so supportive of me, and I have tried to be equally there for her. We even have Netflix parties together to try and recreate the nights we spent here at the Bristol. That ritual has become very important to us.

Our last night at this theater together created something between us. Some sort of bond. I am certainly no believer in mysticism, or even the supernatural, but I think a pact between us – Brianna and me – and the theater was formed that night, in our desperation and fear. The pact, I believe, was this: The fate of one will be the fate of the other.

Right now, the theater is doing incredibly well, and so are Brianna and I. *Our fates are aligning.* I know it sounds ridiculous, but in the screenplay of my life, it makes perfect sense. Screenplays, after all, are full of metaphors, motifs, connections, and parallels. When you examine life, you cannot help but notice that life is full of that stuff as well.

I have decided not to question it. The movie of my life is just beginning its second act. I am in the midst of the rising action, leading to the climax, which I hope is still years away. A lot of runtime remains.

If you know movies, though, you know that the enduring relationships are formed during the first act – the exposition. And that's what high school is. Never disregard the exposition, because the fundamentals of the story are all there. The rising action, climax, falling action, and certainly the conclusion make no sense without the exposition.

Never fear the early parts of the journey.

The Author knows where the story is going.

Special Thanks

My first set of thanks will always go to my family. My wife Aleigha has always been an advocate of my writing, whether it was in the form of screenplays in the past or novels in the present (although she'll be the first to tell you that she's happy I gave up filmmaking for the time being). She was especially great this time around, providing appreciable insight for this book. She is always there to help to remind me in how the characters would actually act and sound.

The other "half" of my family is my son Dawson, and he will always be my single most important mortal driving force. I want him to know that it's always worth striving for more in life – that it's okay to never feel complacent, because life is all about maintaining a momentum. It's all about bettering yourself daily and leaving (hopefully) a good mark on the world after you've left. Well, Dawson is my "mark," and he is the best thing I ever could've done for myself or the world.

Next, I'll thank Sara Seidel, my primary editor. A lot of people read my book (at least snippets) before the final product is released, but I hold her critiques in the highest regard. She's always there to remind me of how readers should be treated and how I should come across to them, and that is an essential part of the writing process.

Sara also hooked me up with the opportunity to shoot this book's cover image at the Farris Theater in Richmond,

MO (a placeholder for the fictional Hudson, MO). The entire theater staff was helpful in my research for this book as well, whether it was in answering questions, giving me a tour of all of the theater's nooks and crannies, or showing me how to run the projector. I have loved this old-school theater for years, ever since I was a kid when my parents would drop me off for a Sunday matinee and then pick me up in time for the evening church service. Guy's fictional love and belief in the healing power of cinema are very much real emotions and beliefs of mine, and I am so happy I was able to incorporate the Farris Theater even more into the release of this book.

An enormous thank you also goes to Izabella Anderson, Brooke Gordon, Carly Thacker, and JT Brown, who all appear on the cover of this book. I want to thank them not only for bringing my characters to life, but for all of the inspiration they provided behind the scenes. I was their high school English teacher; I was their Drama Club sponsor and director; and I was the speaker at their high school graduation. I love each of them, and the rest of the 2020 Hardin-Central graduating class, too. Over the years, I interacted with these graduates on a daily basis, up to three or four hours a day. During that time, I was able to zero in on the anxieties that high school seniors have. Not so ironically, they were the exact same anxieties I felt during my latter high school years. Being around these guys not only helped to inspire my characters, but they helped to inspire the deep conversations that seemed, maybe, "too thoughtful" for high schoolers – like Guy, Brianna, Caitlyn, and Kylie – to have. And that is the whole purpose of this book. I wanted to let the readers, especially the younger ones, know that everything you feel at the all-so-important ages of 17, 18, or 19 is both valid and routine. We're all essentially the same deep down. As "Wade Parker" said in *Petrarchan Girl*, my books may never be studied in universities, but I know they are beloved by a certain segment of people, and that really does keep me going. I count this group as primary among that segment.

Thank you as well to EJ Tangonan, the graphic designer for my cover – an especially important role when I also act as the cover's photographer, as I have for both this book and *Petrarchan Girl*. EJ's incredibly talented, and our relationship goes back to my very first independent film (my film premiere, unsurprisingly, was also held at the beforementioned Farris Theater).

While I'm talking film, thank you to Martin Scorsese, Stanley Kubrick, the Coen Brothers, Woody Allen, Quentin Tarantino, John Carpenter, and Orson Welles. I learned most of what I know about storytelling from them.

Finally, thank you to God for once again granting me another year to live and thrive. There isn't much I can do to repay Him for that kindness, so I simply show my appreciation by writing a book every year.

It ain't much, but it's honest work.

--David Cox
Hardin, MO, October 2020

This is where I am supposed to write a short story. One that relates thematically to the larger story you just read. That story is supposed to be a thinly veiled version of reality – something that gets at the truth of something without addressing it directly. It is supposed to be a humorous take on millennials or a heartbreaking look at a lost relationship or a horrific examination of my state of mind.

I can't do it this time.

I cannot come up with a fictional setting in which to insert these feelings.

All I have is emptiness.

The problem is this – *I lost you.*

I used to see you every day, and you were such an important part of it. I saw you first thing in the morning, and that always set me on the right path. When that normal routine did not occur, my day became a downward spiral. I eagerly awaited the next morning. Maybe tomorrow will be better because you'll be there again. Yeah. Tomorrow will be better. When I see you again, my life will feel normal again. I will feel like myself.

And then tomorrow didn't happen.

I no longer got to see you every day. *It's okay – I can handle this*, I told myself. I just have to go a week. A month. Longer?

Eventually, it became never. How am I supposed to feel like myself again when you – the *defining* part of my happiness – are not a part of my life? I will have to learn how to cope. What else am I supposed to do? This is my new normal.

I missed my opportunity. That was what hurt the most. I just wanted to say "I love you" to your face. Even if you did not have the strength to say it back to me, I would not have cared. I just wanted to finally express myself to you. I don't know what's wrong with me. I would much rather punch someone in his stupid face than actually communicate my feelings in person. But when I had finally gathered the nerve, I forgot that the world does not work in according to my wishes. That is a lesson I should have learned long ago.

It's fine. I can do this. I may not be able to see you, but I can still talk to you. And that is almost as good as the real thing. Right?

It wasn't. Something was lost in those communications. Our hearts did not connect the way they once did. They could not. Our phones may have well as been communication devices between planets. It did not feel the same. *You were not the same.* You said you were okay, but I knew that you were lying to satisfy my worries. You were not okay, just as I was not. In person, you could never have gotten away with such a lie, because you could never have said that to me with a convincing face. With a phone, however, you could lie and smile through emojis.

Everything is fine.

And then the communications ended.

While I was able to survive somewhat through our distanced communications, those too ended after a while – suddenly and without warning. It was a dagger through the heart. There one moment and gone the next. *But what if...?*

No. It was done. I could speak to you no more – only through well-wishing and prayer. I became just another faceless sympathy card.

And now I am left here, where I have been wasting away for years. Stuck and abandoned. You are gone, never to return. I must learn how to live without you. Frankly, I don't want to. That is the truth. I do not want to live a life without you in it.

What am I supposed to do?

Sadness has a way of fueling words. *Write it out,* my inner monologue tells me. That is what I have always done before. This time is different, though. This time I am devastated. I do not have the will, or seemingly the power, to conjure up a fictional story to disguise my anguish. What's the point? It will not bring you back. I always knew you would leave at some point, but I still was not ready for it. I did not even have a chance. No bargains were possible. All I can do now is look at your image and try to remember what it felt like to be around you… to hear your voice… to see you happy and laughing… to feel your embrace. The pictures fail, time after time. They make my chest hurt. They widen the hole within me because they remind me that I will never be the same. You took a chunk out of my soul before you left, and it can never be mended.

I know your life is better now. You are happier now. For that, I am happy. I just cannot help but still feel selfish. What about my own happiness? Is it worth nothing? Am I always secondary? Other people do not have to go through this. *Why me?*

This is not about me, though. It was about you. It always was.

And you are happy now. Hopefully you are not able to feel any of the pain you did while you were here. If that were the case, then that would give me all the happiness I need. I realize my selfishness, but in all truth, I only wanted you to be happy and without pain. If that means that you cannot be here with me, then so be it. I will take that bargain, on your behalf.

Maybe that is not what you would have wanted, but I would still take that bargain.

So what now?

All I feel is emptiness.
Because you're gone.

Goodbye.

Acknowledgments

Birdman. Directed by Alejandro G. Inarritu. Fox Searchlight Pictures, New Regency Pictures, and Worldview Entertainment, 2014.

The Black Keys. "Lonely Boy." *El Camino*, Nonesuch Records, 2011.

Casablanca. Directed by Michael Curtiz. Warner Brothers Pictures, 1942.

City Lights. Directed by Charlie Chaplin. United Artists, 1931.

Goodfellas. Directed by Martin Scorsese. Warner Brothers Pictures, 1990.

The Graduate. Directed by Mike Nichols. StudioCanal, 1967.

Her. Directed by Spike Jonze. Warner Brothers Pictures, 2013.

Hud. Directed by Martin Ritt. Paramount Pictures, 1963.

La La Land. Directed by Damien Chazelle. Summit Entertainment, 2016.

Lady Gaga. "Always Remember Us This Way." *A Star is Born*, Interscope Records, 2018.

Paper Moon. Directed by Peter Bogdanovich. Paramount Pictures, 1973.

Pink Floyd. "Breathe." *The Dark Side of the Moon*, Harvest Records, 1973.

Rebecca. Directed by Alfred Hitchcock. Selznick International Pictures, 1940.

Silver Linings Playbook. Directed by David O. Russell. The Weinstein Company and Mirage Enterprises, 2012.

Sorcerer. Directed by William Friedkin. Universal Pictures and Paramount Pictures, 1977.

A Star is Born. Directed by Bradley Cooper. Warner Brothers Pictures, 2018.

Touch of Evil. Directed by Orson Welles. Universal Pictures, 1958.

Vertigo. Directed by Alfred Hitchcock. Paramount Pictures, 1958.

The Wages of Fear. Directed by Henri-Georges Clouzot. Vera Films, 1953.

Whiplash. Directed by Damien Chazelle. Sony Pictures Classics, 2014.

Made in United States
North Haven, CT
03 September 2025